Willow Creek
Summer

Willow Creek
Summer

Kathleen Wiebe

COTEAU BOOKS
TWENTY-FIVE YEARS

© Kathleen Wiebe, 2000.

Edited by Barbara Sapergia.

Cover painting by Ward Schell.
Cover design by Duncan Campbell.
Interior design by Karen Steadman.
Printed and bound in Canada by Transcontinental Printing.

Canadian Cataloguing in Publication Data

Kathleen Wiebe, 1963
Willow Creek Summer
ISBN 1-55050-169-0

1. Mennonites–Juvenile Fiction. I. Title.

PS8595.I263 W55 2000   jC813'.6   C00-920163-7
PZ7.W635 Wi 2000

10 9 8 7 6 5 4 3 2 1

COTEAU BOOKS
401-2206 Dewdney Ave.
Regina, Saskatchewan
Canada   S4R 1H3

AVAILABLE IN THE US FROM
General Distrubution Services
4500 Witmer Industrial Estates
Niagara Falls, NY, USA 14305-1386

The publisher gratefully acknowledges the financial assistance of the Saskatchewan Arts Board, the Canada Council for the Arts, the Government of Canada through the Book Publishing Industry Development Program (BPIDP), and the City of Regina Arts Commission, for its publishing program.

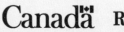

For Susanna and Peter,
whose souls are at once familiar and foreign to me.

ZWIEBACK

Gnarled old fruit trees in our backyard garden bristled with winter-bare branches. There from the time when Orchard Road ran through the countryside, the trees were now mostly ignored. They grew miniature cherries and wizened apricots that only the birds would eat. But in spring the trees blossomed like burning bushes.

In a brick split-level house, set on the very last lot of our subdivision in the little country town of Homer in Niagara's Golden Horseshoe, my mother, Alma Wiens, boiled water in a kettle polished to a mirror's shine. She pushed back a strand of auburn hair that was straggling too close to her eyes. Steam streamed up to cloud the kitchen window. My father, Werner, sat at the kitchen table. His black hair, shiny from Brylcreem and thinning a little at the top, was combed back from his forehead. My mom poured my dad a cup of instant coffee. He took a noisy sip, and placed the cup not gently onto the table.

I had my eyes on the fresh cinnamon rolls, shiny

with egg white, cooling on the kitchen counter. Though my mom said I should wait a bit longer, I pulled one of the buns apart and popped it into my mouth.

"Tina!" was all my mother said, and then my sister, Mary Anne, walked through the front door and dropped her boots on the tiled breezeway floor.

She untied her belted coat and smoothed her pink sweater over her swelling stomach. My father didn't look up, just took another noisy sip and opened the newspaper. He refused to look at Mary Anne, especially at her risen belly, but I couldn't keep my eyes off it. Week by week it swelled up and out, the little thing forming inside her knowing its business better than anyone else in our house.

With the pregnancy – illicit and sinful by Mennonite standards, but curious and exciting to me – my sister had become a stranger to me. I wondered if she might have experienced the rapture our minister preached about, and only her body was left behind, like an empty June bug shell, split along the back where the bug crawled out.

"Hi," I said, my mouth full of cinnamon bun. "Are you hungry?" I always was.

"Just tired," she said, and dropped into the chair beside me, panting a little with her mouth open. Mary Anne had inherited the best of both worlds in my opinion – her hair was somewhere in between my parents' red and black, a glossy chestnut brown that glowed in the sunlight. She was beautiful and womanly.

My mother was torn. She cared about Mary Anne and wanted to take care of her, but my father didn't like it when she made a fuss about Mary Anne. So she didn't say much, just put her hand on Mary Anne's shoulder, then went to the counter and fixed her a cup of milky coffee.

I pushed half my cinnamon bun toward her, very generously I thought, and smiled. "Even if you're not hungry," I said. "Your baby probably is. Eat this."

My dad made a rattling sound with his newspaper, sighed loudly, folded the paper up with deliberate movements, then went to the breezeway, where he put on his coat and left the house.

My mom shook her head at me. She did that a lot these days. Mary Anne ate the bun and my mom sat down at the table with us. It was quiet for a while, all of us chewing or sipping, and then I put on my coat and boots and headed out into the February morning.

"I'm going to Willow Creek," I said. They knew I was going there to think about stuff. It's what I always do.

I let myself out the front door and let the screen slam behind me, shutting in the scent of Saturday baking.

The sky was powder blue and the air was cool. The paved street of our subdivision ended just beyond our house and turned to gravel as I headed toward the outer perimeter of town, toward the creek.

Well-kept yards, now covered with a skiff of snow, and tidy houses soon gave way to twisted, unkempt

3

orchards. On the banks of the creek, which wound through farmland from the Niagara Escarpment to Lake Ontario, tall willow trees grew. At my favourite spot, a bottom of land too wet to be farmed, nearly a dozen willows formed a shaded grove, their long branches providing coolness in summer and peace and privacy at any time of the year. Now in late winter the branches were golden yellow, promising soon to bud and be the first of all the trees to burst into shiny green leaves, silken to touch.

I found my favourite tree, its fat trunk split in two near the base. I pulled myself into the tree and sat in a cozy alcove of trunk and branch, and thought about my sister.

I walked into the bathroom once when Mary Anne was in there. This was last November, that boring time of the year when trees were bare and the snow was waiting for Christmas. Sitting on the counter in her jeans and bra, she slid her chin across her shoulder, slowly. She didn't mind me coming in. I brushed my teeth. When I was finished, I said good night and went to walk past her. She reached out with her bare arm and touched my hand with her fingers.

"See how nice and warm skin is," she said to me. "It breathes by itself."

I wasn't sure what she was talking about, but I kissed her cheek. "I like the cat's fur better," I said to her.

She nodded.

A few nights later, Mary Anne came into my bedroom when our parents were at church for a prayer meeting. She sat down on the edge of my bed, laced a bit of my crocheted blue afghan through her fingers. I looked up from my book and saw that Mary Anne wanted to talk. She dropped the blanket, walked over to my bookshelf and touched some of the books. Then she slid into Oma's old rocker, tilted it all the way back, and let it fall forward.

"I'm going to have a baby," she said.

I closed my eyes. Had I heard right? My sister was too young to have a baby. I couldn't imagine her as a mother. Mothers had no freedom.

"In May." She wanted to keep talking.

"Do Mom and Dad know?"

"No, I wanted to tell you first. It's not that easy to tell them."

She told them on a Saturday morning. Mom was warm and flushed from the oven, her hands clean and wrinkled from working with *zwieback* dough. Dad sat at the table, holding a cup of coffee and reading the *Mennonite Herald*. I was sleepy, just out of bed, sitting at the table wishing the *zwieback* would be ready in time for my breakfast.

Mary Anne waited until Mom finished counting the cups of flour. Then my mom started kneading, steady, even, up-and-down strokes. She rolled the dough, paused, and lifted her hands to do it again.

Mary Anne said, "I'm going to have a baby. In May. I've seen the doctor."

The kneading stopped. Mom's one hand held the dough down, the other froze in mid-air. Icicles of gluey dough dropped in the silence. We were all at our mealtime places, Mom kneading no more at her end, Dad silent at his, Mary Anne staring out the window at the naked cherry tree in our backyard.

Mom worked the sticky dough off her hand, rubbed it till most of it spattered the mixing bowl. Then she sifted a bit of flour into her palm and rubbed her hands together until the dough flaked off. She did this twice, methodically, like she did when she had to talk on the phone before she was finished baking. She looked at the dried bits in the bowl and poked at them till they sank into the dough. Then she started kneading all over again, rhythmically, evenly, as if she hadn't heard.

Mary Anne watched her hands move, then looked at Dad. He asked what I knew he would.

"Who is the boy who did it?"

"You know him." Mary Anne looked my dad in the eyes. "He came here for Tina's birthday dinner in summer. Benedict Henry."

My father didn't say anything else, only looked at my mother, who wouldn't look at him.

Mary Anne thought she had to remind him who Benedict was. "He worked for the Klassens for the past three summers. The one from Trinidad."

My mother remained silent, her lips pursed like

6

she was holding pins in her mouth. Then she picked up handfuls of the dough and squeezed perfectly round buns out of it. The same size every time. She pushed one out, plucked it off, plumped it down onto the greased pan, did this until she had a row, then a whole pan, full of the round, smug, dough balls. She turned to put the pan into the oven to let them warm up and rise, and when she turned back she was crying.

I got up and went outside, through the big door and the screen door, shutting them quietly behind me. This was no place for me, with my mother crying and my dad sitting there silent and Mary Anne's stomach about to rise like the little buns.

When her belly grew, people began to talk. The news rebounded up and down Orchard Road until everyone on our street and the whole town of Homer knew that Mary Anne Wiens was great with child. And also that she wasn't married, engaged, or soon to be. In fact, they'd never seen her with any particular boy and certainly not one of ours.

The neighbours were curious and critical. People looked at Mary Anne disapprovingly across the deli counter where she worked at Abe Goossen Groceries. Everybody tried to guess who the father was, but no one actually asked.

Would my parents have answered them with truth? Benedict Henry was what the Mennonites called a darky. The colour of his skin made him desirable in the mission field and fit for work in our farmers' fields, but it did not qualify him as a suitable son-in-law in the town of Homer.

I'd worked with these men in the summertime, picking fruit on my uncle Bruno's farm. One of them called to me picking cherries in the next tree, "Have you ever made love with a black man?"

There was melody in what he said and his words didn't even shock me. He laughed like a rooster crowing.

"Oh, no, no, no!" his friend cawed. "She much too young to make love!"

One of their friends in the strawberry patch sang hymns on his haunches all afternoon. The words I knew, but the melodies were not what I sang from a taped black hymnbook on clean, ironed Sundays.

These men cackled in the summer heat, tropical birds in the sticky fruit trees, perching on cherry boughs far from home. Laughing under the trees åt lunchtime, they touched heads over a Sears' catalogue and dreamed of what they would fly away with.

One day a tall, thin man came to me with a camera in his bright palm and asked me to take a photo. I plucked the Kodak Instamatic off his branch-brown arm and watched the men through the viewer.

Nine men posed for their summer portrait. A few flocked together in the crotch of the cherry tree, the others surrounded the scarred charcoal trunk, holding stalks of green grass or cigarettes in their lips.

Some knelt, their knees sprouting from baked brown orchard earth.

And then the tall man wanted a picture of himself alone, so he touched the others to go away, and leaned into the tree. Green summer leaves and blood-red cherries imprinted my eyelids, while he smiled at me behind his camera and his friends hooted and clapped.

I thought of my family's legacy. In my mother's old photo album there was a black-and-white wedding picture of a solemn couple, taken back in the days of Mennonite life in the Ukraine.

The grim-looking groom in black, trailing two white ribbons from lapel to thigh, stood stiffly beside his square-jawed bride. Her white ribbons drooped from black wedding roses. I could read no expression on their frozen faces.

Would the baby inherit monochrome? Or would it hatch from the eggs of these island birdmen who trailed rainbow tailfeathers?

I liked to sit and think like this for a long time, but though the February afternoon light was bright with the promise of spring, these late winter days were still short. When the sun dropped to the horizon and the sky went pale green and rosy, I knew it was time to head for home. I climbed down reluctantly. As I walked, I hoped my dad wouldn't be too upset and that we would have a nice Saturday evening.

I let myself in the front door, pulled off my hat and ran my fingers through my short brown hair. I hadn't inherited my mom's red or my father's black, just something dark and in between. The kitchen smelled delicious. I peeked into the oven and saw my mom's *zwieback*, sitting plump and round in orderly rows on the pan, slowly turning golden. Saturday was for cleaning and baking. My mom always made enough buns to tide us over well into the following week. It was my dad's Saturday chore to buy the groceries. When I walked into the kitchen, he was standing at the open fridge door unpacking brown paper bags. My mom and Mary Anne were nowhere in sight.

"Look what I got, Tina. Your favourite."

"Everything's my favourite, you know that, Dad."

My dad wanted to be friendly and act like there was nothing wrong, and that was all right with me. He unpacked the mild white farmer's cheese I liked so much and showed me a loaf of sliced rye bread from Abe Goossen Groceries.

"Worm bread!" I exclaimed, happy to see that he wasn't in a bad mood anymore, and we both laughed, remembering the first time he made me a cheese and rye bread sandwich. I was sure that the caraway seeds in the rye bread were worms, and I refused to eat until my dad poked one out for me and crushed it between his thumb and forefinger and let me smell its pungent, foreign smell.

Cheese and rye bread sandwiches were our special

treat, eaten with my mom's dill pickles during the second period of *Hockey Night in Canada*. Another Saturday tradition.

My dad's favourite team was the Boston Bruins, a bunch of scrappers, which made them an unlikely choice for a pacifist Mennonite. Mine, whichever team housed my player of the month. As I developed an eye for the good-looking players, I liked watching hockey with my dad more and more. I was looking forward to tonight's game. With all the tension in the house, we didn't seem to get many opportunities to relax and enjoy ourselves.

The timer buzzed and my mom bustled out of Mary Anne's bedroom. She gave a quick look at my dad to see if he was still mad, then she turned off the oven and pulled out the pan of freshly baked buns. She tried to fluff up my flat hair and said to my dad, "I'll let you finish up in here, Werner." Then she turned to me, "And I hope you won't forget to dust the furniture." Then she disappeared into Mary Anne's bedroom, so business-like that my father didn't even react. I wondered what women had to do when they were pregnant.

My dad nudged my arm with a bag of fruit. "How do you like them apples?" he said, trying to make me laugh. And then he handed me bananas and a dozen oranges and for a while we worked companionably putting everything away. Then, without even being told twice, I got out a dusting rag and the Lemon Pledge and did the dusting that used to be Mary

11

Anne's job but had fallen to me now that she was busy growing her baby.

After a quick Saturday dinner of sausages and fried potatoes, my mom said she needed a rest. Sometimes she would sit with us during the Saturday night hockey game, doing needlework instead of watching, shaking her head at the size of our first intermission sandwiches and rolling her eyes when we spilled crumbs onto the newly cleaned carpet.

"Tonight Mary Anne and I are going to do a jigsaw puzzle," my mom told us, and headed down to the downstairs rec room with Mary Anne. My dad and I went into the living room and turned on the TV, he with a cup of coffee, me with my imagination ready. As the familiar anthem filled our ears, my father slurped his hot coffee, and I sat back and pictured myself at the arena.

My fantasies always started out the same. Seated near the boards, just far enough back that I could get a good view of the whole rink, and perfectly situated for what happened next, I would be reaching into my coat pocket for a piece of gum, or money to buy a pop, when I'd get hit in the head by a puck, shot over the boards by my favourite hockey player at the time.

Who was, at the moment, Mario Tremblay, a tall, dark Montreal Canadien with an unruly mop of black curls and a nasty temper, a true Harlequin Romance character. The heroic force of his slapshot knocked me unconscious, and I would not waken until the hospital, where I would open my eyes to see his own anxious eyes peering into mine. He would be beside himself with concern, horrified at my bruises, painfully aware that he might have just unwittingly injured his soul's one true mate. I would tell him weakly that I was just fine, although I couldn't stay awake much longer than to receive his bouquet of flowers and an ardent, accented apology.

It would be all over the news the next day. The mid-week game announcers would discuss it during intermissions, and they would interview Mario about it, and he would declare his undying love to me on national television.

The hockey hero fantasy was always pretty much the same. Only Mario's expressions of love varied from time to time, or how ardent he would be. Sometimes he would kiss me, a sweet, apologetic kiss with his finely-shaped Gallic lips.

I spent hours at this, occasionally alternating Mario with other dark-haired and broad-shouldered heroes, while my dad cheered at the goals and groaned at the failed saves. Tonight, however, I couldn't muster up much enthusiasm for the fantasy.

We ate the ritual sandwiches, and by the middle of the third period I was yawning and starting to fall asleep. My mom and Mary Anne went to bed before we did. No one said "night night," and I wondered if everyone was mad at everyone, only pretending they weren't.

NAPOLEON'S TORTE

It was my mother's fault that Benedict had been invited to our dinner table. I didn't know if my father would ever forgive her for it.

My mother, Alma, didn't look any different from other Mennonite women her age. She went to church on Sundays and was a member of the Ladies' Prayer Group. She baked, cooked, cleaned the house, sewed our clothes, and even quilted sometimes. In summer she worked in my uncle Bruno's orchard to make extra money and to help her sister, Lena.

Where other ladies stayed far away from the off-shore workers, my mom wasn't afraid of them. She never called them darkies, like her sister did. She didn't stare at their ivory teeth and yellow palms the way the other women in the packing shed did. She often brought pie, made with fresh sweet peaches, to share with them at coffee break, and she asked the names of the tiny countries they came from – Trinidad, Tobago, Jamaica, Dominica, Antigua, St. Lucia. She didn't treat them like she was a missionary and they were heathens.

Something about these men intrigued her. The Mennonites were, after all, a nomadic people, and other places interested her. She told me, much later, that she befriended Benedict on Friday night when he came to town with his fellow workers. The farmer they worked for drove them to Homer once a week to do their town business. They waited in line at the Farmers Credit Union to cash their paycheques, then headed across the road to Art Goossen Groceries where they bought rice and beans, chicken, potatoes, salt, sugar, and bottles of Coke.

The whole atmosphere of the grocery store changed when they entered. They shopped in groups, chattered in their bright shirts, discussed every purchase seriously, teased each other, and laughed all the time.

All of them except Benedict, my mother said. He shopped alone and didn't even smile. He looked so sad and lost, my mother told me, that she knew he was lonely for family.

Spontaneously – my mother liked to act on impulse – she went to him when he exited the store ahead of his laughing friends and invited him for Sunday supper. It was my fifteenth birthday and we always celebrated with a family *fesbah*, a simple, homemade dinner eaten late on a Sunday afternoon.

Mary Anne and I were surprised when he showed up. He brought me a gift, a book about Trinidad, and he was dressed in shiny black pants and a grey-and-white striped shirt that he wore loose over his trousers. He smiled all the time and his smile was like sun in his dark face.

My mother served fried farmers' sausage, home-made buns, sliced Colby cheese, potato salad, cucumbers in sour cream, dill pickles, and a *Napoleon's torte* for dessert. I was kept busy watching his black fingers break the white *zwieback* delicately, spread it with butter, and bring it to his generous lips. He ate slowly, unlike our people, and he talked the whole time, not shy at all, brimming with stories of his home, their dogs, pigs, and chickens.

He told us his family lived by the ocean and his father was a fisherman. Their house was built on stilts and last year Benedict had painted it green with the money he made picking fruit. I don't think I said anything the whole meal, unusual for me. I couldn't believe that he lived on the same planet as we did.

My mother served the *Napoleon's torte,* my favourite dessert, a cake made of crepes layered with custard. I ate two pieces and saw that Benedict liked it too, because he ate it fast and didn't even tell one story while he chewed. He drank his coffee black and my mother had to go to the cupboard for sugar, because he liked his coffee sweet, which none of us did.

After the meal, we sat in the living room. When it was time to go to Sunday night church service, my father asked if he would come along. Benedict refused. He said he wanted to go home and get ready for the week of hard work on the farm, but he said it so nicely that my father didn't even raise an eyebrow when he mentioned that he was Catholic. That was stranger to me than the colour of his skin.

"What was Benedict like?" I asked Mary Anne. We were in the bathroom, where we spent a lot of time together. I liked to practice acting in front of the mirror, rehearsing for the day I would get chosen for Canaan's spring musical. Mary Anne, by this time, was big and pregnant. She sat quietly on the floor, resting, her back straight against the door, barricading us in. No one disturbed us here.

I wasn't interested in boys. From watching the way the cheerleaders acted around boys, I figured that boys stopped girls from doing what they wanted. Around them girls acted dumb, like they couldn't be smart and have boyfriends at the same time. I knew I was never going to be satisfied with one of our Mennonite boys. Some day I'd go far away and forget all about Orchard Road and Young People's meetings on Friday nights after choir practice.

Mary Anne didn't answer right away. She was deep in thought, twirling a strand of hair between her thumb and forefinger.

"What was he like, Mary Anne?" I asked her again.

"Not like the boys at church," she answered, and I knew exactly what she meant. Our boys sat in the back pews and refused to sing. They whispered and snickered at the back of the church. Sometimes heads turned and people looked at them disapprovingly. A couple of the old ladies on the other side of the church where the unmarried ladies sat together glared at the boys and shushed them with fingers across their mouths, but the boys didn't listen. Boys could get away with being bad, but girls had to obey.

"He was quiet," she said. "And sweet. We went for walks around Homer in the dark on Friday nights when he came to town to cash his cheque and buy his groceries. We met at the grocery store, when I was done work."

"Weren't you supposed to be at Young People's?" I asked, thrilled at her daring.

"Well, Mom and Dad never asked, and I didn't lie."

We smiled at each other. I raised my eyebrows in the mirror and laughed.

"One Sunday afternoon," she said, "I rode my bike to where he lived, an old camping trailer set up in one of the orchards. It had a canvas pop-up roof and it smelled musty. When I got there I was hungry. He fried an egg for me and sprinkled it with pepper. Then he cooked some rice and the whole trailer smelled good."

"He knew how to cook rice!" I was impressed. In the Mennonite world, only women worked in the kitchen. The only time my dad ever cooked was when my mom was sick, and even then he usually just heated up leftovers.

"Then he squeezed lemon into a pitcher, added water and sugar and ice, and let me drink it."

Did she like his strangeness? Mary Anne had never been farther away than Winnipeg to the west, on a family trip, and Ottawa to the east, with her grade ten class.

"He was more like us than I thought he would be," she said, reading my mind. "His English was like Low German. Sometimes I understood him perfectly and other times the sounds were familiar, but I had no idea what he was saying."

"Did you like it?" Despite the threats of eternal damnation, I suspected that I'd enjoy sex one day. Maybe that was why I didn't like boys. I was afraid I'd be too hungry.

She laughed, looked at me hard. "It?" She laughed again. "What do you think?" Mary Anne smiled at me.

I laughed too, without opening my mouth, smiling as wide as my lips would stretch, squeezing my eyes tight at the picture of them in my mind.

It felt strange to talk about this. Part of me wanted to feel guilty, but then Mary Anne took my hand and put it on her big belly. "This doesn't have to happen to you, Tina," she told me quietly. "It's just me. I have to be different."

"The baby must love swimming in there," I said. "Her dad lives on an island in the ocean, after all."

Mary Anne smiled at me.

"Does he know?" I asked her.

She shook her head. "He was gone before I knew, and I don't have his address. Anyway," and what she said next shocked me, and thrilled me at the same time, "he has a wife and son at home."

I thought of the connection between my sister here in Homer, a small Mennonite town in dull, grey, southern Ontario, and Benedict and his family on a green and gold island in a tropical sea. Their baby built a bridge for me and I set one foot down first, and then the next, and began to walk straight ahead, away from the place where I was born.

CANAAN COLLEGE

Mary Anne was eighteen and I was fifteen. She had graduated from grade twelve and I was in grade ten. I couldn't imagine why anyone would want to have a baby. I still thought of myself as a child.

Mary Anne always did what she wanted, even when she was a kid. And she always got away with it too. Not me. I always got into trouble.

Until now, my life had been simple and narrow. I lived with my family in a Mennonite subdivision, contained within the parallel and perpendicular roads of Homer. I knew what I had been taught. But I was developing a vague sense that there was more to life than the neat lawns and straight roads of my town suggested. The orderly rows of pews in our church hid a tangled, crooked world behind. I had memories hidden away in secret, shaded spots where I didn't dare look. But Mary Anne's baby began to change all that.

Geography was my sister's best subject at school; maybe that was why she did it.

In her last year of high school, Mary Anne got an

"A" on an essay she wrote about our ancestry of wandering Mennonites. She traced their path from Switzerland and Holland and Prussia to the Russian Empire, the United States, the Canadian prairies, the Niagara Peninsula, and to Mexico, Brazil, and Paraguay. A bunch of hippies is how she described them to me, living off the land and helping each other, but she didn't mention this in the essay. I thought of them more as gypsies, always looking for a better spot to live. My mother reminded us both that they moved because of religious ideals, and often because of persecution at the hands of other religious people who thought the Mennonites were breaking too many rules.

I knew about rules. High school was full of them. I went to a private Mennonite high school called Canaan Christian College. Kids came from all over Canada to get a Mennonite education in this big stone building, built in the 1950s by churchmen in the fashion of the Mennonite working bee. Hard work was one of the rules of the Mennonites. Holidays, and whether Mennonites should take them, were a topic of discussion in Sunday School. "The SS," I called it, but my mother said that was not funny.

Neither was Canaan. We had to wear black jumpers that came to our knees over blouses with collars, and we couldn't wear clear pantyhose except on the last Friday of the month, which was dress-up day. They said it was to discourage fashion competition among the students and to create an environment of equality between the wealthy and poor Mennonites. I found it boring and restrictive.

Jeans, T-shirts, sweatshirts, and boots were my usual wardrobe. I felt half-naked wearing a dress all the time. The boys were always trying to lift our skirts, and some of the girls wore fancy underwear so they'd be prepared for exposure. I stayed far away from boys, for fear they'd do it to me, but they didn't seem interested in what was beneath my skirts. I was glad, but also felt left out. This kind of attention was paid to the more popular girls.

Canaan College was well known for its spring musicals. Mennonites loved to sing and were good at it. I desperately wanted to get a part, but I just wasn't popular enough. So I blended into the woodwork and tried to be a good student. We studied all the usual subjects, plus Bible, Mennonite history, and German, and we had to attend Chapel every day and sing in the choir.

I was bright. Memorization came easily to me and I wasn't afraid to open my mouth in class. The popular girls grudgingly accepted me, especially where algebra coaching was concerned, but I remained a nobody until Mary Anne's pregnancy gave me momentary star status.

I knew the instant that the news hit school. Morning chapel was over and we were pushing our way down the wooden hallway to the grade ten lockers. My cousin, Lorraine Neufeld, walked right up to me and stood behind me silently while I spun the numbers on my combination lock.

She was my mother's sister's daughter. We'd grown up together, spending summers in her dad's orchard and packing shed while my mother helped out on their farm. Though we'd spent much time together as children, we had never really managed to like each other.

Lorraine was the youngest girl in a family of boys who were all grown up. Where I was short and stocky, she was tall and thin, and she wore her shoulder-length blonde hair in a different style every day. I'd go to bed in my mom's metal curlers, raising sores on the tender skin above my ears, to emulate Lorraine's ringlets, but my hair was too straight, and by lunchtime I always looked like I'd walked though an autumn drizzle.

I easily outshone her in class, though, and got a secret thrill when she asked me to help her with her math homework. How could someone so pretty be so dumb, I wondered, and helped her every time she asked.

She must have been the bravest of her gang and even so she was hesitant. It wasn't a common thing; unwed pregnancies were rare and shameful. Since I was certain that she wanted to talk about Mary Anne, I made it easy for her.

"I'm going to be an aunt in May," I heard myself make a joke, "just like my Tante Tina. Maybe you guys could start calling me that. Tante Tina. A new nickname."

Lorraine looked at me with wide eyes, twirled a fat curl between two slender fingers, turned to look at her friends on the other side of the hall, and faced me again. "Don't you think it's disgusting, Tina? A sin? The unpardonable kind? The kind you go to hell forever for?" She'd obviously been listening in Bible class.

Lorraine was the kind of person who bought it all. She thought that as long as she went to Chapel and had the right answers in Bible class, and hemmed her jumper at the right length, and went to church on Sundays and Young People's and choir practice on Fridays, she would be saved. It didn't matter that she cheated on science tests and treated me like I was a leper. Maybe she was afraid Mary Anne's sins would jeopardize her own chances in heaven.

A very deep and rich and fat anger bubbled up inside me. I heard thunder in my ears, blood pounded in my fingertips, and even as the words shot like cherry bangers from my mouth, I remembered how dumb she was. "Yeah, well, I'd rather be in hell with my sister than in heaven with hypocrites like you!" I shook with rage and I gasped for breath as if I'd just run down my driveway to catch the school bus.

The hallway was as silent as church during altar call. Lorraine's eyes got as big as dinner plates. I'm sure she was surprised at my anger; I was. I added, shouting now, "Be careful, Lorraine, your face is gonna disappear in a minute if you don't shut your mouth!" My urge to punch her in the teeth was distinctly non-Mennonite. I knew I was going to hear about this from my mom.

Mr. Rempel, a biology teacher that I'd never credited with much sensitivity, barrelled out of his classroom then and ran to where Lorraine and I stood. All the hairs on my body stood straight up like the spring wheat my mother planted in a wooden bowl for Easter.

Mr. Rempel looked at both of us and I knew that he knew too. He looked at me the longest. Beneath the one huge eyebrow that ran continuously across his forehead and inspired the boys to mock him by holding a comb on top of their own eyes, his eyes were sad.

"Maybe we should all kneel down right here," he said, and I could see that he cared to help me, "and pray that our words be forgiven before they are written forever in the Book of Judgement."

My hairs were relaxing again. Instead of thunder, I heard rain. I looked at Lorraine who, thankfully, had shut her big mouth and lowered her eyes. I knew she was going to drop to her knees in a minute and part of me wanted to ask for forgiveness for my yelling. Lorraine was my cousin, and even though she had been mean to Mary Anne, I knew I should be nice to her. She was probably just embarrassed to be part of such a bad family. Mr. Rempel put a hand on both of our shoulders, and I knew I should submit and be good. If I didn't, he'd call my parents, and my father would shake his head quietly, disappointed in me, and my mother would cry.

But then I thought of Mary Anne, so soft and motherly looking, her body rising like bun dough in a big bowl. Why did Lorraine want her in flames, burning eternally in hell, far from cool water? No matter what, my sister didn't deserve that.

I stiffened my spine and shook Mr. Rempel's warm hand off my shoulders. I closed my eyes for a moment against the glare of hell's flames and the fear of getting a detention from Mr. Rempel for talking back. "There is nothing I said here," I heard myself enunciate as I'd always imagined I would if I got a part in the spring musical, "that I do not wish recorded in that book."

Then I shut my locker and left the girls staring and Mr. Rempel shaking his head. "I'm going to German class now," I called over my shoulder. "I don't want to be late."

BANANA PLATZ

I didn't go home after school that day, but asked the bus driver to drop me off at Anna's house. My friend hadn't been at school, and I wondered if she was sick. Anna Block and I became friends when she and her four red-headed brothers and four strawberry blonde sisters moved to Homer from a Mennonite colony in Mexico. Her big, noisy family lived on a fruit farm beside Lake Ontario, in the farmlands outside Homer. Their farm wasn't big enough to hire migrant workers, so Anna and her brothers and sisters worked hard almost all year round, picking and packing fruit on the family farm.

But today it was March, very early spring, and the Block kids were playing in the barn and riding bikes in the orchard and teasing the dog. Anna wasn't in the yard, so I knocked on the front door of their grey stucco house. From the outside their house didn't look big enough for all of them, but the rooms inside were large and the ceilings high. All the girls slept in one bedroom and the boys in another, like a dormitory. It was surprising how well everyone got along.

Anna's mother answered my knock. She was a tall woman with a low, sweet voice and big hands. Though she'd had nine children, she was still beautiful and she wore her golden hair in a delicately complicated coronet of braids. She was always calm and regal. She treated her kids with respect. She acted as though she really liked them, and their friends too.

"Come in, come in!" Mrs. Block welcomed me, her English heavily accented with the Low German that was spoken in the Mennonite colonies. "Anna had a fever today. But she's starting to feel better now. Let me see how she is."

I walked in and sat down at their huge kitchen table, on a bench that stretched the length of the kitchen, while Mrs. Block went to the bottom of the stairs and called Anna. When she returned to the kitchen, she poured two glasses of homemade juice. It was cool and sweet and tasted like peaches. Anna came down then and sat across from me at the long kitchen table.

"Hi," she said quietly, and sipped from her juice glass.

"Drink, drink," her mother said, and rested her big hand on Anna's head. "You need to cool your fever."

Usually Anna's hair was smooth and neatly braided into two perfectly even braids that hung from just below her ears to the middle of her back. All her sisters wore their hair like this. At night before bed was the only time the girls wore their hair down. Then they sat together, with their mother, combing out each other's hair in rippling waves of red and golden curls. Today, because she'd been sick, Anna's straw-coloured hair was loose and wavy. It was a bit messy. Anna looked sleepy. She gave me a little smile. She was a gentle, quiet person. Not like me. We didn't say much, just sipped our peach juice. In that peaceful kitchen, I forgot momentarily that everything in my world was wrong.

All the burners on the stove were covered with steaming pots. They boiled and hissed. I could smell something roasting in the oven. Anna's mom picked up lids, stirred contents, replaced the lids, pulled the roast from the oven, drained the meat juice from the pan, and reserved it for gravy. Then sat down beside Anna, across from me, her generous hands folded on the plastic tablecloth. The house was unusually quiet. For a moment all the members of Anna's big family were somewhere else. She put the back of her hand against Anna's forehead to check for fever, then turned it over and placed the palm on the top of Anna's head, briefly.

Then she turned to me. "How's your sister?" she asked.

I looked down at my glass of peach juice. "She's fine," I answered, my peace destroyed. "She's just fine, but everyone else is not. Everyone."

"Including you?" she asked me gently.

My lips twisted into a funny kind of smile, and I

looked down at the tablecloth. I nodded my head and kept nodding. One of Anna's little brothers called out from a bedroom upstairs, but Mrs. Block ignored him for a second.

"A woman has to be fine when she's making a baby. That way the baby also will be fine. Soon everybody will be good again. You'll see."

Anna's mom's words were comforting, but I was worried about my sister going to hell.

"Don't think so much about it all," Anna's mom said to me. "You're still a girl."

A girl, but I was already fifteen years old, and not getting any younger. And not a very good Christian. Would I go to hell too?

Anna's brother called again. "Worrying never helped anything," said Anna's mom, getting up from the table and turning down the heat under one of the bubbling pots.

Easy for her to say, I thought. But I felt better drinking her peach juice and sitting at her table and hearing her words.

"Here, eat this," she said, cutting a wedge of her delicious banana *platz* and sliding it to me on a chipped white plate. She was the only Mennonite mother I knew who baked with bananas, something she learned in Mexico. "You have a long walk ahead of you." As I left the kitchen and walked toward the door, she said, "Come back on Sunday when Anna's better. You girls have such fun together."

Anna nodded and smiled, drained her juice glass.

"But I'll see you at school tomorrow first," she said.

I nodded, turned to go, and said goodbye.

Platz in hand, I left the house chewing and nearly bumped into Anna's dad, who was finished work for the day, heading to the house for supper.

He took off his hat when he saw me and gave me a little bow. His hair was black and thick, and when he smiled I saw that he had straight white teeth. "Did you leave anything for a hungry, hard-working man?" he asked. His voice was so pleasant and his smile so genuine that I forgot for a minute to be confused and sad about Mary Anne.

"I'm pretty sure I left you a little piece," I said. "You're lucky!"

He laughed and bowed again to make me smile and waved goodbye with his hat. I took the back way home through the Blocks' orchard down one of the dirt roads along the creek.

I stopped beside a willow tree to finish the *platz,* and when the cake was eaten, I crawled under the tree, whose slender golden branches draped over the water like long hair, and stuck my hands in the creek-water. The water was cold on my warm skin. I dropped my head to look at my hands under the water and became sad again. I didn't know what to think. Was Mary Anne bad? Was the baby bad? Was I bad?

Fat, hot tears plopped into the water, and little rings of brown creekwater spread out from my tears, getting larger and larger until they disappeared. A plump yellow carp did a lazy roll as he swam by. Anna's mother said everything would be fine, but she was just a farm wife. All she knew how to do was make babies and banana *platz*. Although she did both very well and maybe she knew something I didn't.

I walked home slowly, thinking.

When I got home from Anna's place, my dad was standing at the sink in his dark blue work shirt and pants. A pot of water on the back burner was steaming at full boil and he was peeling potatoes with his sleeves rolled up. He said hi, and sighed.

"Where's Mom?" I asked. I couldn't understand why my dad was cooking.

"I don't know," he answered. "But I'm hungry, so I thought I'd start the potatoes. They take a long time to cook."

I nodded, turning down the heat underneath the pot, like Anna's mother had done. "How was work?" I asked him.

He smiled and laughed a funny laugh before he answered. "Well, you know the General. He doesn't abide a lazy man."

My dad worked at General Motors in the neighbouring city of St. Catharines. He worked on the assembly line, sticking doors onto car chassis all day long. He always said he worked for the General. That was his little joke.

"One of the guys on the line was sick today, so we had to work harder." Then he brightened. "But it was so nice that I ate my lunch outside. A couple of us guys had a small Bible study. Everybody else thought we were crazy sitting outside in winter reading the Bible."

"It's not really winter any more. It's just barely spring. So, you're not so crazy after all."

He smiled a little, then quartered the potatoes and dropped them into the boiling water before drying his hands on my mom's apron that was hanging by the oven.

"I need a shower," he said. "The General made me sweat today."

"I'll go find Mom," I called to him. I knew where she'd be. Down the road, past the edge of our subdivision where the land dipped and rolled down to the creek, I found her. She stood there without moving, her face into the wind, her eyes shut like she was tasting something delicious. Behind her the willow trees shook their branches like clean laundry on a sunny line. Though it was early spring, the branches were golden and their smooth buds promised leaves one day not too far away.

I didn't say anything, just slipped my hand into hers. She turned toward me and squeezed my hand, not so hard that it hurt, and then we walked slowly back to the house. In the kitchen she picked up the lid and tested the potatoes with a fork, then dropped the pot lid with a twirl.

"Did you start the potatoes?" she asked as she went to the fridge and pulled out a package of ground beef.

"No, it was Dad," I replied.

She nodded her head, looking a little surprised and impressed, as she chopped onions and added them to the hamburger. Soon the kitchen was filled with the smell of sizzling meat. She rummaged around in the freezer and pulled out a plastic bag of bright yellow corn kernels. "This is the end of last summer's corn," she said, setting another pot of water to boil. Everything seemed normal again.

When the food was ready and I had set the table, we called my dad and Mary Anne for dinner. As usual we all bowed our heads and said, "God is great, God is good, let us thank him for our food. By his hands we all are fed, give us Lord our daily bread. Amen." We said it in unison, but each of our voices was different. My dad's was lowest and Mary Anne's the highest. My mom and I were in between.

I was always tempted to make food rhyme with good, and had to try not to laugh. I just rattled off the words because they had to be said before I could eat. I didn't think it was right to thank God for our food. It wasn't by his hands that we were fed, but by my mom's – who prepared the food – and by my dad's who worked hard for the General to make the money to buy the food.

But it was fun to chant the poem, and I always added a ringing "Amen!" Today's was so loud that my dad lifted his eyebrows and my mom shook her head.

It made Mary Anne smile, and that felt good. After all, Mrs. Block had said it was important for a pregnant woman to feel happy.

Then we passed around the mashed potatoes and the seasoned ground beef. Mary Anne got up once to find a cucumber in the fridge and cut it up for salad. Babies needed vegetables, I knew that too.

ROSA

That week at school we had a special chapel. We always did at this time of year, sort of like spring cleaning. Instead of the usual twenty minutes, Chapel lasted for an hour. They brought in a special minister from California who really knew how to turn on the taps. He wanted everyone to tell how we'd been saved. Already this morning a lot of students had gone to the front to share. Everybody's stories of getting saved were different – some people had been saved at summer camp, some at a revival meeting, others at home, at a Billy Graham crusade, and at school. In the back, Mr. Rempel let out a big hallelujah.

Anna sat on my left, and Rosa, a new girl from Paraguay, sat on my right. They didn't tell their stories, but it was only because Anna was quiet and shy and Rosa didn't speak good English yet, not because, like me, they hadn't been saved.

I felt so alone listening to all the testimonies. Everybody around me accepted it – church and God, how to get saved and ensure a place in heaven.

Something in me refused to believe it. I couldn't see how to get Jesus into my heart, and I had begun to pay dearly for this unbelief with fear. I was having a hard time falling asleep at night. I wanted to pray for comfort, but the picture of a bearded Jesus, knocking plaintively at my heart's door, always made me laugh. Because of that I knew I was condemned to eternal damnation, not a pleasant thought.

My cousin Lorraine went up to the pulpit to tell her story of salvation. She would.

"I was at Camp Bethesda," she said, slim and confident up front. "One of my camp counsellors shared his testimony. God must have spoken to me through his words, and I accepted Jesus into my heart."

If I knew Lorraine, she got saved because she thought her counsellor was cute. They probably knelt together, with his arm around her shoulders, while she accepted Jesus. It didn't seem to make a difference in her life, she was still mean to Rosa and called her Frankenstein, not even behind her back.

I shook my head, and thought, instead, of Rosa sitting so quietly beside me.

Rosa's family had come to Canada only a year ago. They lived in a wooden farmhouse on an old orchard stuck in the middle of a new subdivision. In the spring the cherry and plum trees flowered in their yard and grew fruit that Rosa's mother canned in jars and stored in their basement.

Rosa came from a Mennonite colony in Paraguay. Her family was poor. She was the oldest of five and her mother was pregnant again. Rosa had to be a mother to her sisters and brothers. Her own mother was too tired. Rosa's mother had ulcerated varicose veins in her legs and blue circles under her dark, sad eyes. She was pale and quiet, and I heard my mother say once that if she survived the next baby, it would be a miracle.

Rosa's father was a tyrant. I often watched him at church, in his ill-fitting Sunday suit, a fat, striped tie hooked beneath his too-tight collar. I saw how he became furious with the children in the church pew, pulled at their earlobes until the children dissolved, red-faced, into tears. Sometimes, when this tactic failed to keep the child quiet, he took the child into a broom closet in the basement, reserved for Sunday morning discipline sessions. This practice, if not encouraged, was certainly overlooked. Sometimes the offending child didn't return to the pew at all. After church I'd see a pale, pinched, tear-streaked face through the window of their ancient station wagon.

Rosa told me stories of her home life. Her father never shouted, but his silences were more terrifying than rage. Sometimes he would diffuse his anger by kicking the family dog. Other times he pushed and shoved their mother, and if the children got in his way, he would flail at them with his ham-sized fists, sending the child careening into corners of the lop-sided farmhouse.

I befriended Rosa partly because I felt sorry for

her. I could understand Low German, and that was her first language. Mostly, though, I was Rosa's friend because she loved to swing and to tell stories. She talked to me in the Mennonite dialect I'd learned by listening to the women, in the kitchen after dinners. The seriousness of Mennonites was always transformed by this earthy dialect, and I loved to listen to it.

Rosa came from a small Mennonite settlement at the edge of the Chaco jungle in Paraguay. She had never seen a swing before. There was an old rusty swing set up at the back of our schoolyard. She thought it was a chair at first. Her eyes lit up when she saw me swing.

In the air, she discovered freedom.

My mother felt sorry for her. One Sunday she asked Rosa's parents if she could spend the afternoon with us. We ate together. Rosa had no manners. She devoured her lunch – soaked her *zwieback* in my mother's gravy, sucked on it loud, and didn't lift her head until her plate was empty. She was shocked when my mother offered her a second helping, looked at me and my sister before she nodded. For dessert my mother served last summer's canned cherries with vanilla ice cream. Rosa ate all hers, spitting her pits noisily into the glass bowl before my mother had even finished serving. My parents exchanged looks over Rosa's bent head. My mother shook her head and sighed.

After lunch that day, we walked to the schoolyard. We had all afternoon until *fesbah,* an early Sunday

40

dinner before the evening church service. We made a beeline for the swing.

We took turns swinging; mostly I listened. Rosa's stories were fantastic. I shut my eyes and listened to her bright words. Jungle trees, snakes as fat as pigs, blue butterflies, warm rain, rats in the house ceiling. She lost a cousin and three chickens to a tarantula once. Wild boars and star fruits intrigued me. Her father had been bitten by a scorpion, and he had got so angry he squeezed the life out of it before it let go of his skin. Then he howled, once, and left the house until daybreak. He returned with a thumb as big as a banana.

Rosa had the gift of storytelling. For me it was better than reading a book. The beauty and terror of her tales transformed her into an exotic creature. Without me, Rosa had no audience for her stories, and she treasured my ears.

She spoke Spanish and promised to teach me to count to ten; we started pumping our legs in time, chanting Spanish numbers. By *quatro,* Rosa had achieved good height. At *siete,* she whizzed above my head. Her skirt flew in the breeze. At *ocho* I saw the bruises. The backs of her thighs were mottled black and purple, like marbles. One streak was turning green. I felt a shiver of apprehension on my skin. Instantly I felt nauseated. "Rosa!" I called. "Stop!"

She looked at me inquiringly, but straightened her legs and glided to a stop.

"Rosa," I said. "What happened to your legs?" She

stared back at me, as if gauging my concern. Her lips moved without sound and I thought maybe she didn't understand.

I asked her again in German.

"Was ist dir passiert?"

She closed her eyes. For a second she looked as old as my grandmother. Resigned. She held her lips together and blinked.

I looked at her and saw a tear pool in the corner of her eye. It hung for a moment, sparkled like a star, then she tipped back her head and the tear ran down the side of her face and disappeared into her hair. I didn't know what to say, wanted my mother, wanted an answer, dreaded the answer.

She shook her head to rid her face of tears. Her hair waved in a breeze that ruffled the puddle beneath my toe. Now I was curious. I knew this was serious.

Rosa spoke in German, "I fell."

I didn't believe her.

"I fell down the stairs into the basement," she continued, "because my father pushed me."

I had been in their basement once. Old wooden steps like ladder rungs led to a concrete cave at the bottom of their old farmhouse. The basement smelled of must. My throat caught with that smell. For some reason I liked it, but I couldn't breathe deep down there.

Rosa told me then that her mother sometimes locked them in the basement when she was too tired to stand their noise. In one corner a sump pump surged on and off. One wall was covered with shelves where her mother stored canned cherries, jars of strawberry jam, and peach preserves. A wringer washer stood beneath a cement ledge where they stored clothespins, a box of detergent, and an assortment of dirty rags and old socks that no one ever washed. It was Rosa's job to do the laundry. She always had to go straight home after school to help her mother.

"But why did your father push you?"

She continued as if she hadn't heard my question. "My father was angry because dinner wasn't ready and he was hungry. He only had an hour before he had to go to a church meeting and there was no dinner, so he got mad at me. I should have fried some potatoes after school, but I was reading a book."

"He grabbed the book from my hands," she told me, "and threw it down the basement stairs. When I ran to the door to see where it landed, he pushed me too. 'First the book and then the girl!' he shouted at me." Rosa's voice was strangely flat, devoid of emotion, like a robot. "I didn't hurt myself and when I landed on the ground I went to look for my book. He was shouting at me not to touch the book, but I didn't listen."

I was horrified, impressed at Rosa's determination in the face of her father's rage.

"I found the book. It had landed face down into a puddle of water. I picked it up, dried it on my skirt. Then I sat down on the bottom step and tried to find my spot."

I pictured her father, furious, and Rosa defiant. He beside himself. Flailing at the little boys who gathered, silent and scared, to watch the scene between Rosa and her father.

"He started to come down the steps toward me. I turned around to look at him and then I threw the book at him. It hit his face and he stopped and stared at me. And then I knew I would get it. He got to the bottom of the stairs, held my shoulder, got a length of rubber hose from the washing machine, and hit and hit and hit me."

We sat on the swings, dragging our feet in the rutted gravel below.

Rosa slid carefully off the swing.

"I fell," she said again, "down the stairs, you see." And she got up, a little stiffly, and started walking slowly across the schoolyard and back to my house.

"It's time for *fesbah,* no?" she asked. "I like your mother's cooking."

Suddenly I remembered where I was. For a moment the Chapel was quiet and I wondered if the preacher had asked me a question. I didn't know what to say. Then the minister began to plead. He stood at the front, his eyes closed, face pointing heavenward. He asked, he begged, he cried for people to let the Holy Spirit lead them to the front, to share their stories of salvation.

I wanted to stand up and tell everybody in Chapel about the bad things that I knew happened in basements, behind closed doors, in secret, when on Sundays everybody sang so loudly, in four-part harmony, and the preacher prayed for fifteen minutes at a time. I wanted to say shame on you to Lorraine and her friends for being mean to Rosa, and for saying my sister was going to hell. But Lorraine was one of the most popular girls at Canaan College. Almost everybody agreed with her opinion of Mary Anne. I knew no one would listen to me.

Finally chapel was over. We all got up out of our seats and started pushing and shoving to the doors and down the hallways to our lockers and our next class. It didn't seem like anyone else found anything out of the ordinary. Only me.

"I'm glad that's over," I said to Anna and Rosa who flanked me as we left the Chapel.

"I thought it was all right," said Anna. She never made a fuss.

"It was interesting," said Rosa, her eyes big. "I didn't know there were so many ways to get saved."

They were my friends, but they didn't really understand me. "English class is next," I said. "My favourite!"

Literature was my favourite subject because it didn't have anything to do with the Bible. Although here at Canaan College, even literature could become a problem – many Mennonites didn't approve of books. It was all right to read the Bible, but it was not proper to read novels. Unless they were sanctioned by the church, and only when all the work was done, and never for too long.

But I was a bookworm. I read when I first woke up. I read while I ate breakfast, I read at school and after school in the willow tree, and I read at night in my bed, under the covers to hide it from my dad. He tried to stop me, but since that was impossible, he said I could only read books from the church library. I didn't particularly care for those books – their characters were sappy; in Christian books people acted as they should, rather than how they would in real life.

Even the Bible had better stories than those Christian books. I scoured the Bible for exciting passages and found plenty there to interest me. Treachery, bravery, deceit, action, adventure, romance, passion, and sex. During church services, I learned to tune out the preacher while poring through the Bible – it looked like I was paying attention to the sermon, but my mind was far, far away – and I was never bored in church.

I discovered that books were gateways, channels, sources of great light. They fueled my burning curiosity about the world; books opened the sky and gave me wings.

In my grade ten English class we were introduced to Roman and Greek mythology. But the courses at Canaan College were designed to teach the follies of human ways, and we always read a passage from the Bible at the end of each class.

The class became quiet immediately as Mr. Siemens, a black-moustached man who could have easily been a drill sergeant if not for the pacifist creed of the Mennonites, drew the day's lesson to a close. "These Greeks and Romans created their gods in their own images," he said. "Look how they aren't godlike at all, but so very human in their actions, committing adultery and deceiving their subjects."

I put my hand up. I didn't think he'd agree with me, but something in me compelled me to speak.

"It seems a bit more realistic," I said. "I mean the God in the Bible doesn't seem to allow for human error, like these gods do. Adam and Eve made one mistake, and God couldn't forgive them. At least these gods were a bit more human."

Mr. Siemens smiled at me sadly, and shook his head. "Here we have the classic human error," he said to the class. "Expecting God to be like the feeble human. The one and true God is not a man, and he would never act like one."

"But why does he insist on punishing us for being human, when he created us and gave us the power of choice?" I asked, knowing the answer Mr. Siemens would give.

"It was humans who chose evil, in that passage in the garden of Eden that you referred to earlier," he answered. "Not God. He created us perfect."

"But he created Satan," I insisted, "and Satan is evil."

"And some humans choose to follow that evil one," he said carefully and clearly, so that I knew he was warning me personally. "And they will suffer for their wrong choices, just like the people who didn't heed Noah when he told them of the flood."

"Well, that wasn't fair either," I said, softer now, squirming in my seat, thinking of the poor people drowning in the flood, calling out to Noah to pick them up, and Noah, inside the ark, ignoring their terrified pleas. "I mean, if God had appeared to all of them personally like he had to Noah, then they might have listened too."

Mr. Siemens looked distressed. He shut the book of Greek myths and walked to his desk. He picked up the Bible and held it close to his chest. "I recommend that you read this as the Word Of God. It is not ours to understand God's words, only to accept and obey them. I think you would be better served by reading devotional works which attempt to interpret God's words, rather than atheistic writings which only lead to trouble."

He let the threat hang in the air and the bell rang. The class, which had been silent, erupted into chatter. Anna and Rosa picked up their books and waited for me at the door. "Lunch time," said Anna. They didn't say anything about my comments in class, but they were nice to me. I traded one of my mom's cinnamon buns for Anna's banana *platz*. She said she was sick of her mom's baking, and tossed a braid over her shoulder.

"I'd never get sick of your mom's *platz*," I said, and ate my piece happily and wished that school would be over soon.

ROMANCE

The week passed slowly, and finally Saturday's work was done and Sunday church was over, leaving a whole afternoon open and free. On this Sunday afternoon there wasn't much happening at our house – Mary Anne and my mother were doing a puzzle, my dad was watching football. I headed for Anna's house.

It was a nice April day, warm enough to wear a light windbreaker. The sky was clear and the lake was dark blue, like my mother's eyes, as I walked past the edge of our subdivision to Anna's house.

After Sunday lunch Anna's parents napped – my parents didn't do this, and I suspected that this was why I had only one sister and Anna had so many siblings – and we had free rein of the house, the kitchen, and the television. At two p.m. the station from Buffalo broadcast old black-and-white horror movies.

As I arrived, Anna's oldest sister, Bertha, was filling two of their mother's huge mixing bowls with popcorn. She poured melted margarine into the white drifts of corn and sprinkled salt like snow. Anna turned the TV on. She and her brothers and sisters and I lay on the living room floor, devouring popcorn as the movie began. To accompany this salty treat was Anna's mother's specialty, fruit punch made in two-gallon pickle jars. We all had glasses of it.

The movie was about a man whose girlfriend had been killed in a car crash. He happened to be an amateur mad scientist, so he saved her brain and transferred it into his dog. He was so in love with the memory of his girlfriend that he took the dog everywhere he went – to work, to the grocery store, on his vacations. He talked to the dog like a lover, slept with it in his bed.

We loved it, hid our eyes in the gory parts, shrieked over the sexy bits, stuffed ourselves with popcorn, and sucked on our salty fingers.

When the movie finished, I noticed that Bertha and her boyfriend seemed to be very inspired by the romantic theme of the movie. They were pressed against each other like two pancakes stuck together with syrup. They gave us the impression they wanted us to go away, so we retired upstairs into the room below the eaves that Anna shared with her sisters. The younger girls and boys went outside to play.

I loved Anna's bedroom. It was all corners and crooked walls and sloping ceilings. The stovepipe passed through on its way out the top of the house. The girls slept on metal beds, each with a different headboard. Anna's was shaped like half a wagon wheel, with spokes that radiated from a sun in the centre. We sat on her bed, spread with a homemade quilt, and devoured Harlequin romances the same way we'd just binged on popcorn.

Anna read aloud and let me unbraid her hair. I combed its ripples with my fingers. It was thick, as slippery as the sash on my mother's dressing gown, and it tickled me.

"Let's eat some of your mother's *platz,*" I suggested.

"I'm still stuffed," protested Anna, who looked glamourous with her hair down. "Let's write books." She put her Harlequin romance aside, and rolled onto her stomach.

"O.K. My guy's name is Marcus," I said to Anna, flopping down next to her. "And my name is Hilary. I'm staying in a castle on the coast of Cornwall, I think it's in Wales. There's a big storm and the cliff below my window is crumbling. I've always hated Marcus because he thinks I'm only a kid. I'm eighteen! He calls me Bones. I hate him. The castle is in danger of tumbling down the cliff, and he happens to be below my window, because he was scouring the beach for his brother's fishing boat. His brother died in a storm more than ten years ago, but Marcus refuses to believe he is dead. He goes down to the beach during every storm, and calls out over the waves to his brother. In a flash of insight, I realize that his soul is deeply grieved over the loss of his brother and I want to comfort him. When he rescues me in the driving rain, his hands slip and our lips crash into each other."

"That was pretty good," said Anna, "particularly the slippery lips."

I laughed. "You next."

"I'm Brooke," said Anna, swinging her mane of hair. "His name is Ricardo. I'm from London, a buyer for a lingerie company. Ricardo is one of two twin brothers who run an Italian fashion house. His wife left him for an English polo player and so he hates all Brits. Especially me, because I remind him of his wife, who had long red hair and green eyes too. I'm a strong businesswoman, and tough. I fall in love with his brother, Roberto, just to spite him. Ricardo is so jealous that he starts being nice to me just because he wants to win me from his brother. They've been competing since they were children. In the end, I see a photograph of their mother, a green-eyed redhead, who died giving birth to the twin brothers. I fall in love with Ricardo because I feel sorry for him."

Anna's romances were always better than mine. Her imagination was bigger, and she understood human nature better because of her huge family.

"You will be a famous writer when you grow up," I told her. "You can call yourself Anne McDonigal. You can live in a high-rise in New York City and wear leather boots with mini skirts."

Anna laughed. "That's what you want to do. I just want to go to university and become a pharmacist. Every town and city has a drug store and I could get a job anywhere I wanted to."

"But your stories," I insisted. "You have a talent.

You know what they say. You shouldn't hide your light under a bushel."

"I want to help people," Anna told me, seriously. "I want to help old ladies sleep better at night. I want to help people with arthritis have less pain and cure babies of their teething pains."

"Why don't you be a doctor, then?" I wasn't sure that Anna was going to live up to her potential.

"Because I don't want to chop people's heads off and dig out their brains."

"Oh, darling, I must know. Do you still love me like you did before?"

Anna barked at me, twice. We dissolved into giggles and crashed into each other in the soft middle of her metal bed. Her hair cascaded over both of us like a waterfall. Then she sat up straight and braided her hair, without a mirror, into neat, symmetrical braids with a perfect part.

When she was done, we went downstairs and cut thick wedges of her mother's banana *platz* and we ate them off the plastic tablecloth at their long kitchen table.

My dad picked me up from Anna's house and drove me home for dinner. Our house was quiet after Anna's place. I wished I had more brothers and sisters, and then I remembered that there would soon be a new baby in our house.

LAUGHTER

As Mary Anne's pregnancy progressed through the spring, my father softened toward her. Maybe he knew too, like Anna's mother said, that you had to be nice to a woman when she was growing a baby.

One day at suppertime, Mary Anne announced that, though she was hungry, she couldn't eat much at all because her stomach was so squished.

"Maybe we should make her some mashed *postanack*," said my dad, with a wink.

"*Postanack!* What's *postanack?*" I asked.

"Parsnip," my mom said. "Why would that help?"

"Because," my father said, and I saw him try not to smile, "because mashed *postanack* tastes so terrible, that if Mary Anne only ate a little she'd be happy!"

We all laughed. It was nice to hear my father make a joke, even if it wasn't a very good one.

Then my mother added to the fun by remembering some Russian and Low German names for things.

"Or maybe," she said, "Mary Anne would like some *bockelzhon*."

"Tomatoes!" my dad translated. "How about some *schmaunt supp?*"

"That sounds horrible," I said. "What is it?"

"Hard to explain," my mom said, and burst into laughter.

"Platz!" Mary Anne added.

"Borscht!" I shouted, rolling the "r" like a real Mennonite.

"Glomms!" my mom threw in.

"No, I think she'd prefer some pickled *arbuz!*" This from my dad.

"What's that?" asked Mary Anne, laughing with the rest of us.

"Pickled watermelon," my dad said, and made a face that made Mary Anne laugh even harder. Me too.

"They used to make watermelon syrup," said my mom, holding her side. "That's what they used when they couldn't get sugar."

"Very creative," said Mary Anne. "I wonder how they discovered that!"

"Very sweetly," said my dad.

"Very messily," said my mom. And we laughed some more.

It wasn't very funny, but it felt good to laugh with everybody. Just laughing together was funny. We hadn't done it for a while.

"Maybe Mary Anne would like some *jebrodne eeahcheke,*" said my mom.

"Only just a little!" added my dad.

"What's that?" asked Mary Anne suspiciously.

"Fried potatoes," said my mom and dad in unison.

"Now that I might like," said Mary Anne, rubbing her stomach.

"That I would definitely like," I said, "particularly if you call them French Fries."

You would have thought that I was a professional comedian the way they all laughed about that comment. My mom actually started crying, she was laughing so hard, and Mary Anne grimaced and said she had to stop laughing because it was pinching her insides.

Then she gasped a little as though it was a pretty good pinch. When my mom saw her face she stopped laughing and said it looked like all that laughing might have made the baby think it wanted to get out and join us.

It was a full-blown spring day when the baby came to live with us. Mary Anne brought her home from the hospital on Mother's Day. It was the second Sunday of May and Orchard Road was living up to its name. Every backyard blossomed with remnants of the orchards that once filled this street, and now gave the street its name.

Cherry trees, plum trees, apricot trees, apple, pear, and peach trees brought fragrant, pastel clouds to earth. I loved this time of year when the air was warm and sweet. I wished I was a bee so I could dive into the sticky centre of every flower.

Our house was unnaturally quiet. Normally relatives and friends, church members and neighbours would have fallen over themselves to phone, to bring handmade gifts, knitted booties, tiny quilts, and peppermint cookies for the new mother, and *koletten, hlopstje,* and other delectable dishes to tide the family over while the new mother regained her strength.

But Mary Anne's situation was different, of course. People greeted my mother if they passed her on the street, but their enthusiasm was cloaked with disapproval. My mother's sister, Lena, dropped by one day when Mary Anne was still in the hospital. I was glad she didn't bring Lorraine along. Aunt Lena came to the door with a frown. But she asked nicely about Mary Anne and when my mom said the baby was perfect, her sister's lips curved into a smile. She left a casserole with my mom. Anna's mother sent some early season rhubarb pie with Anna's oldest brother, Helmut, who drove over by himself. I hoped Anna would come over too, but I was glad for the pie and swallowed my disappointment with a sweet taste of the tart dessert.

My father skipped church service to bring Mary Anne home. My mother was home anyway – she didn't like to go to church these days. She said she couldn't stand the critical stares of people who had known her since she was a little girl. They didn't look her in the eye anymore. She had no patience for the sagging spinsters who approached her with tears, clutching worn leather Bibles to their bun-dough breasts, assuring her in *Plautdietsch* that they were praying for us. I still went to Sunday School, because my father said I should, but I felt tension too. It was as though they thought our whole family was bad, not only Mary Anne.

But sun and warmth and quiet anticipation of seeing the baby put this afternoon in a good light. My father rounded the corner carefully and parked the car gently in our driveway. Mary Anne sat smiling in the front seat, holding the tiny bundle that was the baby. It was so nice outside that we all went to sit in the backyard under the cherry tree.

In its shade the air was sweet and the bees were buzzing. Mary Anne handed the baby to me. The baby slept and my mother cried. My father stared at the baby, took his big hand, with his fingers cracked and black from his job at General Motors, and touched the baby's forehead. She woke a little and her mouth opened wide, soundlessly, and then she squeaked and her eyes fluttered at his touch. Mary Anne lay on the grass. She dozed and I held the baby.

Just then a car drove into our driveway. My mother looked up, surprised, and my father went to greet the visitor. It was my dad's aunt, my Opa's sister. I called her Tante Tina. We shared the same name.

In her hands she held a gift-wrapped package. Tina was a tidy woman, big and compact at the same time, with a wide shelf of breasts. She wore her long, steel-grey hair twisted into a fancy bun. She laughed often and loudly, despite a life that had been hard and full of work. She had also – unusually for Mennonites – been a single mother, and when her widowed brother died in a work camp in Siberia, she took his daughter and raised her as a sister to her own child.

Tina worked hard when she first came to the Niagara Peninsula with her brother, my Opa. Their parents had died in Siberia during Stalin's reign of terror. She spent long days in the St. David's canning factory during the summer and cleaned house for city women in the winter. She was the best cook in all the branches of my family and made the fanciest baking. There was always something in her oven and she was generous. She married a widower long after she could not have children anymore. This man was a good carpenter. He fixed up her old brick farmhouse, built a circular staircase from cherry wood he cut himself from their backyard, and made a big wooden swing under the oak trees beside her house.

Her husband died, her children grew up, and now she lived alone in the middle of some old orchards. She kept chickens, and a cow and its calf, made her own butter and bread, sold eggs, and planted a huge garden in the summer.

I respected her and I admired her strength, her courage, and her independence. I also loved to eat her plum *platz*, warm and sticky and sweet with buttery *ruebel* on the top.

Her child's real father was shadowy in the dark pages of unrecorded history. There were two stories. Some of my relatives believed she had been raped by a Nazi soldier while escaping from Russia to Germany during the Second World War. This violent image shocked me, made me appreciate my own safety in our square and neat subdivision. Others said Tante Tina had fallen in love with this German soldier, but her brother, my Opa, had refused to let them marry.

It was hard to picture Tante Tina, now as sure and strong-willed as a mountain, under the thumb of her brother, but it was a long time ago. Way back in Europe when they were refugees, when they walked, with a skinny old horse and rickety cart, from their Mennonite colony beside the Dnieper River, through Poland to Germany, tagging along with the defeated, retreating German army. Maybe that's what made her so strong now.

She stepped into the shade of the cherry tree. The serenity of our family circle was not lost on her. "Looks like the holy family," she laughed. "I think I see a halo around that one," she said, pointing at Mary Anne.

Mary Anne woke up then. Tante Tina had a voice like a train whistle. When she laughed, her breasts heaved like Lake Ontario in a strong November gale. My great-aunt handed Mary Anne the parcel.

"I made it for your baby," she said. "And to remind you that you are not the first mother to have a baby without a father." I wasn't sure if she was talking about herself, or about Mary, the mother of Jesus.

It was a quilt, sewn with minute stitches, by hand, of course. One side was as pink as the cherry blossoms above our heads, and the other was green like the newborn leaves. The stitching formed the shape of roses. It was a work of art and I envied it, wanted it for myself, to sleep with on the nights when I dreamed the dream that I hated, and the foghorn kept me awake.

Mary Anne liked it too, I could tell. She smiled and her eyes were like the sky.

"Tell me, Tante Tina," the euphoria of childbirth made her brave, "did you miss never seeing your German soldier again?"

Tante Tina laughed, more a bark than a laugh, shook her head at my sister and pointed her finger at the baby. "Save your questions for your little girl. She will be a mystery to you."

Then she looked at me and said, "And you, *Tinche,* you will come and stay with me in the country this summer, so I can teach you how to grow vegetables and to make a quilt like that for yourself. Then you don't have to get yourself into trouble to get such a nice present." And then she laughed, hard, at her own joke, and woke the baby who cried louder than my laughing aunt.

Mary Anne named her Christine. Right from the start I thought of her as the Christ child, but I didn't say that to anyone. I was learning when to keep quiet. Chris was born perfect, the colour of whole wheat bun dough. She was warm and caramel, golden like corn syrup. Her puckered pink lips were rose petals. Her head was covered all over with fine black curly hair like cotton wool. Mary Anne didn't mind if I rubbed my huge hands over her soft head.

"Her hair feels like my cat, Mary Anne."

She laughed and kissed the soft spot on top of Chris's head.

I loved the baby, but I was glad I was not my sister.

Mary Anne was a member of the church. She had been baptized when she was fifteen with six of her friends. One Baptism Sunday they all wore black choir gowns, naked underneath except for their bathing suits. The minister called each one separately into the church's baptism tank that swung open like a door to a secret room in a haunted house. He held her two clasped hands in his and asked the baptismal questions. Mary Anne answered, "Yes, and I do." Suddenly he dunked her backwards.

Because of those vows, she had to make a public confession of her sin, the sin of having Chris. One Sunday night in June, when Chris was a month old, Mary Anne had to sit way up front where the preacher usually stood, while rows of accusing faces stared at her. All the church members were there to vote on Mary Anne's forgiveness.

Every pew was filled that night, faces ashamedly

interested. A few of the men sat low in their seats, rubbing their chins. My cousin Lorraine sat with her mom and dad on the other side of church from us. She kept looking over at me, but I ignored her. People glanced over to where my parents sat. I knew everybody sinned, but my sister's sin was the kind that couldn't be hidden.

The minister preached about how we were all born in sin, even a tiny baby like Chris. That's why we had to ask Jesus into our hearts and get baptized and go to church, because we were bad from the start. I couldn't believe that perfect, innocent Chris could be sinful.

I wished I could think of myself as innocent and perfect too; once I must have been just like Chris, newborn and unspoiled. But I'd heard the sermons about sin too often and had come to believe that I was bad. I longed to be good, though, and I tried everything they said. I asked for forgiveness from my sins. I asked Jesus into my heart. I followed the rules – I didn't drink alcohol, didn't swear, didn't dance or go to movies. But it didn't make me good. I was still mean to my mom and complained about my chores and I didn't like my Opa. I couldn't believe some of the things they taught us from the Bible, and I just couldn't stay saved. I wondered how to start over, to remember that I was once as perfect as Chris, but I couldn't do it.

Sex outside of marriage seemed to be the worst crime someone could commit. Dancing, lipstick, movies, and reading novels could all lead to sex. That's what my Sunday School teacher, with her hair pulled back from her face and twisted into a tidy bun, told us. That's why Mary Anne was up front. That's why the pews were packed on a Sunday night, when usually they were only half filled.

I guessed they imagined the seduction. I did. I knew I shouldn't, but I loved to think of it. I saw him gentle with my sister because he was her first man, his head dark against her pale skin, tickling her I think, making her laugh because that's how he was different from us.

I kept my eyes on Mary Anne. Her mouth was soft and round, directing a circle of breath at the baby in her arms. She looked small but strong sitting way up front, and I wondered how my brave sister could sit there so calmly when I was on the edge of tears.

When the minister was finished preaching, he turned to Mary Anne. "Are you sorry?" he asked her.

She nodded, once, then looked down at Chris again. The way her face dropped, it looked like she was acting sorry for her sins. The minister seemed satisfied because he turned to the congregation. "Shall we forgive her?" he asked, indicating that people should raise their hands if they agreed.

While the minister was counting all the hands, I watched Mary Anne. She shifted her position to allow Chris to lie more comfortably. She smoothed the baby's blanket and tucked it in around Chris's body. It looked to me like Mary Anne didn't really care whether she would be forgiven or not. How could she be so brave?

If my mom didn't like to go to church before, she refused to go after Mary Anne's public judgement, even though the vote was in my sister's favour. I continued to attend with my father, but my mind wasn't on the sermons.

Instead I explored the Bible for my favourite passages. I liked some of the stories in the Old Testament, but I found the visions of the Apocalypse in Revelations terrifying. The Bible was full of dreams and beasts and prophecies and giants. People lived for centuries. It was fantastic and dramatic – lamentations, punishments, visions, and seductions. It was like the Greek and Roman mythology we had studied at school.

One day I discovered an old Bible in the church library that the librarian probably didn't even know was there. If she had known what kind of a Bible it was, she would never have let me read it. It contained the Apocrypha – Tobit, Judith, and First and Second Maccabees – a collection of books I'd never seen before in the Bible.

Tobit was full of fantastical events – a woman, pledged to seven bridegrooms, a demon named Asmodeus, a rotting fish, and a cure for blindness.

The Maccabees were full of the gore and guts of war – pagans, bloodbaths, looting, sacking, burning, desert raids, and torture.

But the book of Judith was a real find! It was about a woman with the mind of a general. Judith was a fine, upstanding widow who seduced an army captain, Holofernes, to save her people, the Jews. Holofernes was attracted to Judith because she was so beautiful and respectable, but Judith was too smart for him. When he invited her for a date, she got him so drunk that he passed out. That's when Judith cut off his head! And showed it to the Jews, who got all riled up and started attacking the Assyrians under Judith's direction. Basically, she saved the day and that's why they wrote this book about her.

I asked my mom about the Apocryphal books. "Why wouldn't they include them in the everyday Bible? Why don't we learn about them at Canaan?"

"I've heard them say it's because these books are not historically accurate," she replied.

"Oh, and the other stuff is," I laughed. "All those beasts and angels wrapped in clouds with rainbows on their heads and the seas of blood in Revelations!"

I was afraid that she would think I was being blasphemous, but she didn't even "Oh, Tina!" me.

ONKEL THIESSEN

After the baby was born, I felt like I was more grown up. More mature than my classmates and church friends, certainly, and more experienced in the ways of the world.

But my mother still sent me on errands, like I was a child. Usually she asked me to deliver food to old or sick people. It was her way of being helpful, and maybe she thought it was good for me to talk to the old people of our community. I liked the candies, cookies, and stories I got as thanks, and I did find it interesting to learn the history of my people.

On this particular Saturday afternoon, my mom sent me with *borscht* and fresh *zwieback* to an old man we called Onkel Thiessen. I was in the middle of reading a book, angry at the interruption, even if it was for a mission of mercy. I grabbed the food from my mother's hands and slammed the door behind me, ignoring her thank you.

Onkel Thiessen lived in a house that looked like the three little pigs' brick house, at the far end of

Orchard Road where the square lines and neat lawns of the Mennonite community disappeared into the tangle of old, gnarled orchards. As I walked and left the ordered subdivision behind, I was happy to be outside and sorry that I'd been mean to my mother. I vowed to be a better daughter, and I intended to pay for my sins by being nice to Onkel Thiessen.

Onkel Thiessen's false-brick house was almost entirely obscured by an elaborate mandala of leafy vines and creepers. Today, in early June, the leaves were small and bright green. I said a secret password before knocking. The blue paint on the wooden door was dry and peeling. Some paint chips flaked off onto my knuckles, but the old man didn't answer. I found him in his garden, working on his hands and knees, moving quickly along the rows, planting carrots, peppers, and green beans. The neighbourhood children were afraid of him. His voice was hoarse and breathless, probably because he rarely spoke to anyone.

I saw him before he saw me. For a minute, from the back, he looked like my Opa, and I was afraid to call out. I wanted to go home. I didn't like the thought of being alone with this old man.

Onkel Thiessen sensed I was there. He turned and greeted me with a toothless smile. I helped him to his feet and held out my mother's gifts. He was pleased to see the hearty soup made with beets, cabbage, tomatoes, and dill picked fresh from her garden and dried, and her golden-crusted, feathery-soft *zwieback*, perfected after years of baking. I felt sorry for Onkel

Thiessen, who had never married and had never enjoyed a woman's fine cooking and baking. He smiled at me and, in Low German, asked me inside. I was ashamed that I hadn't wanted to come. He obviously needed company.

His house smelled like mildew. He never threw anything away. Boxes of flattened tins and rolled up newspapers, yellow and stiff, filled the rooms beyond the one he lived in. Empty jars lined his windowsills, strung along the wallboards like glass beads. There was dust on everything.

Onkel Thiessen had no family. His parents hadn't survived Stalin's persecution of the Mennonites in Russia. His sister had died in Germany of measles, in a refugee camp where the men and women were separated from each other by old sheets strung up for curtains. His own feet had frozen so badly that he lost two toes on each foot. That's why he crawled in the garden.

He sat down in front of his wood stove in an old upholstered chair, with a bare spot on the seat where the springs showed through, and indicated I should join him.

Sitting in front of this stove, he had told me many stories of the old days in Russia, describing rows of neat farms whose occupants shared the work of building a mill, barns, churches, and the school. The richest Mennonites had large farms with servants who tended to the horses and flat-footed camels to do the heaviest work. The daughters of these wealthy

69

landowners learned to play guitar and to do fancy needlework. He was only a boy then, but Onkel Thiessen remembered the black soil of the earth along the Dnieper River and the warmth of the breezes that brought out the apricot blossoms in April. He told exciting stories too, of revolution and bandits who rode their horses like they were born on them.

After his stories, he offered me pieces of dried orange that were sitting on his window ledge. I accepted, to be polite, and was amazed that the stiff, dry oranges still contained sweet juice.

Despite the dirt and smell of his house, I didn't mind visiting because I lost myself in his stories. They gave me a glimpse into the fascinating world of my Mennonite ancestors. My favourite was about a Mennonite family attacked by revolutionaries in Russia. During the Russian Revolution, these wealthy Mennonites became enemies of the Russian peasants. In a terrible raid by a band of marauding horsemen, a cruel captain lined the family up against a fence and threatened to kill them by firing squad.

I pictured the barns in flames, the horses neighing in terror, the horrified family. Some of them were brave, perhaps, sure of swift passage to heaven, but some must have panicked. At the last moment they were saved by a true and trusting Russian coachman who testified that he'd been treated well by this family and begged the captain to let the family live.

Onkel Thiessen cried when he told this story. Was it his family, I wondered?

Today Onkel Thiessen began by talking about the homestead where he grew up. In early spring, before the ice on the Dnieper River melted, the men cut out great chunks of ice and hauled them home and dropped them into holes lined with straw. This is where they stored milk, butter, cream, and meat during the summer. The ice lasted throughout the summer months, until the nights became cool enough to keep things fresh again. But his idyllic descriptions of life in those days turned sour. Something triggered a sadder memory in his recollections, and he began to reminisce about a time of persecution. His whole family was sent to a labour camp in Siberia where they were forced to work hard, with not enough food. His father had to pull logs from a nearly frozen river, barefoot, and his mother had to wash cold stone floors on her hands and knees until her hands developed chilblains. And still they had to work. And each day they received less and less food. His father, said Onkel Thiessen, survived and returned home as pale and thin as a shadow. He never recovered, but cried himself to death thinking of his poor wife scrubbing and scrubbing the cold stone floors.

I was quiet after this story. The only sound in the room was the ticking of Onkel Thiessen's old grandfather clock, the single piece of furniture that had survived his family's sad history. It never told the right time, but it ticked regularly and rang out the hours tinnily at the wrong times.

Sun on this long, early summer day, streamed

through the kitchen window, illuminating dust motes dancing in mid-air. It was lonely and beautiful at the same time. Then Onkel Thiessen groped on his window sill for orange slices. He gave me one too, and we ate them together, him working at his with his gums and me biting into mine with my sharp teeth. Onkel Thiessen didn't ever tell me how he felt about these events in his past. But I could tell that he was sad and a little confused that his life had turned out so, and that he was all alone now.

As I got up to leave, he seemed to return to the present moment, and he looked at me as though he recognized me, and he said, in German, "Your Opa? How is he?"

My Opa! I didn't want to talk about my Opa. My Opa was a strange man, a great embarrassment to me. I didn't know how my dad — who was usually nice — could have come from such a strange man as my grandfather. My Opa was mean and crotchety. He didn't like anyone — not even me, his granddaughter. Once, in Opa's barn, something happened that still scared me. Something I'd never told anyone.

But Onkel Thiessen asked again, like it was impor-tant, *"Wie geht's dein Opa?"*

"Okay, I guess," I answered in English, shrugging. I couldn't tell Onkel Thiessen my feelings about Opa.

"He has had a hard life," said Onkel Thiessen. "You know he lost two children during the *Flucht* and his parents died in Siberia."

But I'd thought my dad was an only child.

"So many children died," said Onkel Thiessen, in German again. *"So viele Kinder."*

I really had to go home then. Onkel Thiessen had given me a lot to think about. As usual, it wasn't all easy or pleasant.

When I got home, I let the door slam shut behind me. My mother was washing the kitchen floor. She indicated I should wait at the doorway until the floor was dry. She sat back on her heels on the white linoleum. "So, was it so bad?" she asked, smiling at me like she forgot I'd been mad at her.

"Well, his house is pretty smelly," I said. "But his stories are like a movie. When he talks, I can see the places and the people. It's like I'm watching it all from a great hill and the steppes are spread out before me."

"Good!" she said to me. "Maybe you will be able to find the good in it all."

I wasn't exactly sure what she meant – Onkel Thiessen's stories were sad, like his life, not good, and the new information about my dad's family was certainly not happy – but the floor was dry and she said I could pass by and I did.

Mary Anne was in the living room changing Chris, who had diaper rash. Mary Anne smeared white cream all over Chris's bottom, and fastened her diaper. Chris was crying a little bit, fussing is what Mary Anne called it. It's what I did all the time too, only in my mind, not out loud.

My dad came in with the Saturday groceries. He

looked in the living room and when he saw Chris, he put down the bags and walked toward us.

"What's the matter, little thing?" *Tleena ding* is what it sounded like in *Plautdietsch*. It was his nickname for her.

She stopped fussing when she heard his deep voice. Her head swivelled toward him and her watery brown eyes focussed for a second in his direction. He put his big finger into her little palm and she grasped it, reflexively, and squeezed. It made him feel good, and he smiled. Then he said a funny little nursery rhyme, in Low German, that I remembered from a far-off time when I was a baby.

"Pita Panna
Sat em amma,
Lot ein poop
en hupte root!"

Mary Anne smiled at that and I laughed. Hard. It was about a little boy named Peter Penner who sat in a bucket, let out a poop, and jumped out again. It was silly nonsense, something my dad rarely indulged in, but Chris brought it out in him.

Babies seemed to do that. They made you speak baby-talk, they made you make funny noises. You just wanted to squeeze them and make them laugh and smile.

And it wasn't that hard.

I thought about what Onkel Thiessen had told me

about my Opa. He had lost two babies. Maybe that's what made him so strange. But even if he was sad about that, and disappointed, it didn't mean he had to take it out on his family. It seemed to me that he should love us more because of his sadness. We could have made him happy. If he'd let us.

I couldn't understand him at all.

THE WITCHES

My experiences with old people continued. The following weekend my mom slipped a jewelled jar of homemade strawberry jam and a couple of roses tied with ribbon into my hands and give me instructions to deliver them. This time I obeyed more willingly, remembering how the visit to Onkel Thiessen had turned out well.

Aganetha Enns and Hannelore Loewen were sisters. One had married and remained childless, the other had stayed home to take care of their parents until they died. What would Mary Anne and I be like when we were old? Who would take care of our parents? I wanted to move far away and never come back. I hoped Mary Anne wouldn't mind.

The two sisters lived together in a tiny wooden house the colour of gingerbread tucked beneath two weeping willows. Their house reminded me of the one that Hansel and Gretel discovered in the woods.

My few quick knocks brought them to the door,

the short, round sister peering around the shoulder of the tall, straight one. They both wore special stockings and Bible-black orthopaedic shoes. They could have easily passed for witches in a book of fairy tales.

I answered their curious stares by announcing myself as Alma Wiens's daughter and handed the gifts to the plump sister. She smiled. Her lips made creases in the bun dough of her face, and she took my hand in her own warm, soft hand.

"Komm, komm," she instructed, and pulled me into their warm kitchen, redolent of baking. "I'm just baking *pfeffernusse,"* the plump one said. "Soon you will eat some."

The tall one shut the door behind me without speaking, and for some reason I felt trapped.

They invited me to sit in the living room, in a soft chair lacy with doilies. The plump sister brought me *platz* made with last summer's frozen apricots and offered me milk. "The *kuchen* are ready not," she said in her German-accented English. "But this I made yesterday."

I said I preferred coffee, and the sisters looked at each other and raised their eyebrows. The short one called me *Kaffee Tante,* and brought me a milky cup of hot coffee.

This I loved, the combination of homemade fruit pastry, and the bitterness of coffee. I munched and sipped contentedly while the sisters fussed with the roses and held the jar of jam to the window and exclaimed over its colour. Were they trying to fatten me up in one visit?

Their living room was full of crocheted spreads, German Bibles, a prayer calendar, a plaque made of dried flowers and sunflower seeds, called *knacksott* in Low German, that read *Gott ist die Liebe,* a German magazine called the *Mennonite Rundschau,* plastic photo albums, and framed pictures of missionary families that our church supported.

I heard them conferring in Low German, but couldn't make out what they said. I understood *Plautdietch* from listening to adults tell stories after dinner, but they were speaking too quietly. From their faces, though, I knew they were arguing. The tall one looked angry, her lips gathered with a drawstring of disapproval. The short sister looked worried. Her hands fluttered like feathers in a breeze.

And then the tall one sat down across from me in a red sofa made of stiff, prickly material.

"Nah ja," she said, and she tried to smile, but her eyes remained angry below the mesh hairnet she wore to keep her bun tidy. "Jesus is not happy mit your family," she said, finally. Her voice was low and accented with *Plautdietsch* and sorrow.

I stopped chewing and stared at her with my mouth full. She really was a witch. I looked around to find the soft and sympathetic sister. She was scurrying from one end of the room to the other, roses in hand, looking for a doily to buffer the vase.

I swallowed and waited for the tall sister to continue.

"You have sin in your *haus,*" she said, "and this Satan loves."

Somehow I wasn't surprised that she knew what the devil did and didn't like.

Suddenly the house seemed hotter, as though the baking oven was overheating.

"We have a baby in our house, if that's what you mean," I said when my mouth was empty. "And we love her very much. You would too. She's just the colour of the bottom of my mom's *zwieback.*"

The fat, round sister cooed and squeaked, made placating noises, then sat beside her sister, a plump blob of bun dough, set on the sofa to rise.

The sisters looked into their folded hands. The older one's lips were clenched so tight they were white.

I wanted to push the witch into her oven, and stuff her bum in good with my feet.

"Suffer the little children to come to me," I said to them, and swallowed the last of my milky coffee. "Red and yellow, black and white, they are precious in his sight, Jesus loves the little children of the world." I sang the last line like we did in Sunday School.

"Ach," the round sister sighed, and seemed to collapse a little, yeast dough that wasn't given enough time to rise before it was moved.

"We will pray for you and your family," said the tall

one, and she seemed to grow straighter, until I thought her head would bump the pebbled stucco ceiling.

I looked around their living room, listened to the clocks ticking and the sisters breathing, and I thought I could see the big leafy rhododendron in the corner telling me to get out now.

The oven timer went off and we all jumped, the sisters a little shamefaced, me right out of the soft chair and into the kitchen, where I found my runners and headed toward the door. It was a race between me and the straight one. I had to get out before she barred my way like the angel who guarded heaven with a shining sword.

The soft sister stopped the timer and opened the oven door. She pulled out a pan of little round peppermint cookies that smelled like ammonia and busied herself with a bowl of mint-green icing that she spread like butter onto the white, warm cookies as I did up my laces. Then she handed me one as I let myself out the door.

I liked the squishy little mint cookies. My mother never made them, so they were a delicacy. But this cookie burned my fingers and I dropped it into the ditch as I ran down the street toward home.

THE UGLY DUCKLING

For all the fuss everyone made about Chris and Mary Anne being sinners, it seemed that our home life should be more exciting than it was. We settled into a routine that revolved around Chris. My mother and Mary Anne were always doing something for her, feeding her, playing with her, changing her, washing her and her clothes, sterilizing bottles, making formula, looking for her soother.

My father joined the choir and a men's fellowship group and went to church a lot more. Anna and Rosa were busy with the school yearbook. I hadn't signed up, hoping I'd get a part in the school play, but I failed the auditions. I felt left out of life. Mary Anne's baby had further blacklisted me at school and, though I still got good marks on my tests, none of the dumb girls even asked me for help. Their mothers probably told them they shouldn't.

I started dreading Mondays. The only good thing was that it was nearing the end of the school year. Finally there was only one more event to endure before I would be free for the summer – Advancement Dinner. The Ladies' Auxiliary prepared a supper in the gymnasium for all the students to celebrate the end of the school year. It was a chance to dress up, and it was very important to be asked by a boy. But I knew none of the Mennonite boys was going to ask me to the supper social.

Despite Anna's braids, she got asked. Despite Rosa's pimples, a Paraguayan boy asked her. As I'd expected, nobody asked me, the ugly stepsister rejected by the prince because her feet were too big. So I went alone and sat between Anna and Rosa and made everyone around me laugh.

I ate the soft white inside of my *zwieback*, and filled the golden crust with mashed potatoes and corn, fashioned a mast from a carrot stick and floated the whole thing down a river of gravy. I chewed the coleslaw and asked people if they liked seafood. Then I said "See!" and opened my mouth. I ended this performance with a rousing rendition of my favourite Low German word, *schnodderkodder* which meant snot rag and was our word for a hanky, while pretending to sneeze a peeled grape out of my nose and into my corner of the white tablecloth.

I had a great time and thought no more of it, but the principal of Canaan College called my mom. He told my parents what happened. Who told him, I wondered? Everybody at the table had been laughing.

The principal said he was very disappointed in me. My mom told my dad, who shook his head and said he was disappointed too. Even Mary Anne rolled her eyes.

"Why can't you just act normal?" she asked. I wasn't really sure what that meant. Was she acting normal? I didn't think so. Was anybody in my family acting normal? I didn't think so. What exactly was acting normal, I wondered.

Nobody seemed to have any answers for me. I felt like I'd been born into a foreign land. My ideas, the ways that I thought things should be done, were not what the people around me believed. I vowed to lay low for the rest of the school year, and to beg my parents to let me go to the public high school in September.

My great-aunt Tina, the one whose name I shared, came to my rescue. The day Chris came home she had appeared, like a Fairy Godmother in the fairy tales, to say she would take me for the summer. She called my mom one night in mid June and made good her promise; she asked my mom if it would be all right for me to spend the summer with her. She said she was starting to feel old and having a pair of young hands around her place would be very helpful. Because she put it that way, my parents thought it was a good idea.

"I'll miss you," my mother said, the needle in her fingers flashing through another baby quilt. "But Tante Tina could really use your help. I know you're bored here, we're so busy with the baby things. You'll have fun on her little farm. She's got cats and a cow and a garden, and she's the best cook in the family."

I thought of what I knew about Tante Tina. She was not like the old women at church, wrinkled and sagging and bossed by their husbands. My great-aunt had been single for most of her life. She'd raised her own daughter and one adopted niece without the help of a man. She was capable, industrious, and multi-talented, and she alone of all my female relatives was respected by the men of our community, who never said her name without nodding their heads.

She didn't go to church, and she had a strange relationship with her brother, my Opa. She visited him, but she didn't seem to like him. Once a month she drove in from the country to see him. She always brought him some of her famous baked goods, fruit *platz* or *schnettke,* and sat with him at the kitchen table, sipping coffee while he ate her goodies. But she refused to enter his house at any other time and, when her girls were little, she never allowed them inside his house. This was a detail my mother relayed with some relish. Even in winter, she said, they had to play outside while she visited with her brother.

Why did she create such a ritual out of her monthly visits, I wondered?

You couldn't ask her something she didn't want to answer. If challenged, she would glare, breathe hard out of her nose like a dragon, and shake her head. Let her get started telling a story, though, and she would weave a fantastic tale. Tante Tina had an appetite for gossip. She loved to chew on the greasy meat of any tale. And she wasn't afraid of the gristle, which we called *gnurpel,* either.

Most of all I wanted to know the story of her fatherless child. Maybe this was the summer I would find out.

"I'll miss you too, Mom," I said when she told me. "But I think I'd like to stay with Tante Tina. I'll work hard and play with the animals and I'll get fat as a pig eating all her yummy food."

My mom smiled. "I'll bet you have a great time. And learn a lot too. Tante Tina is a wise woman. And she loves to laugh."

So it was decided.

THE FARM

The plan was that I would help my great-aunt on her farm from Monday to Friday in July and August and come home for weekends. I couldn't wait for June to finish.

Final exams and essays and locker cleanup signalled the end of the year at Canaan. The last Chapel was long, with graduates tearfully describing their wonderful years at Canaan, how their lives were shaped by God, how we should be thankful for the Christian environment of Canaan College. I ignored it all and read a book behind my Bible. The only part I liked was the music, and I sang harmony in the choruses.

On the last day of June, my parents drove me to Tante Tina's place. Her two-storey brick farmhouse was tucked on the other side of a rickety bridge which crossed a little creek near the base of the Niagara escarpment. She wouldn't cross the bridge in her car and left it parked beside the road. Two old oak trees protected her house, casting cool shadows. The swing her husband had made sat near the breezeway, which was a porch that ran along one side of her house. It was screened in summer and cooled by the breezes that sprang up beneath the two old oaks.

Her farm was small but busy. Tante Tina kept twenty chickens, a cow, and its calf. Cats ruled the straw-filled barn loft. She had five acres of orchard – cherry, apricot, plum, and peach trees – a huge strawberry patch, a garden full of vegetables, and, best of all, a lazy, fat horse named *Schrugge*, which was what Mennonites called a horse that didn't have to work. People came from all around to buy her fruit, her eggs, and whatever homemade specialities she was in the mood to sell. She had learned bone-setting from her own grandmother back in Russia. People came to her to have their muscles massaged and their backs *knicksed*.

Tina made lunch for my parents and me, a typical hot weather meal of *zwieback*, pickles, coleslaw, cheese, and sliced meat. We ate outside in her backyard on a picnic table beneath the oaks. Beside the house, a garden already grew luxuriantly in the heat of early summer, and her small orchard was green and thick with the promise of fruit.

Tante Tina watched me eat my *zwieback* – I had at least three – and she said, "I know Tina will work hard and be a great helper."

I nodded, my mouth full of last summer's pickled beets. When my mouth was empty I excused myself and went to the barn to meet the farm animals. My parents stayed in the shade all afternoon and visited in *Plautdietsch*. The warm summer breeze brought occasional bursts of laughter to me where I sat in the hayloft. Everything felt right here in the barn, the cluck and gurgle of chickens, my lap full of kittens, the smell of dried grass, an empty pen for the horse in winter. I didn't have to worry about what people said. I cuddled the kittens and fell asleep leaning against a hay bale, entirely content and satisfied.

My mother found me and woke me up with a hand on my cheek. "I've never seen you look so peaceful," she said. "Not since you were my little baby."

I smiled sleepily. She picked bits of straw from my hair and smiled at me. "Come say bye to your dad." I cleared my lap of the kittens, who squeaked as they tumbled into the hay, and followed her out.

My dad was already in the car on the other side of the bridge. Tante Tina stood beneath the big tree beside the bridge holding a plastic container full of baked goodies. She handed it to my mother.

"Be good," my father said to me as he started up the car.

"Have fun," my mother added.

I smiled and looked at Tante Tina. She put her warm hands on my shoulders and stood behind me as they backed out of the little rutted driveway.

"I'm sure she won't have a problem doing both," Tante Tina said. I waved until their car disappeared from view. It seemed as though they were going very far away.

The next morning I woke early, but Tante Tina was already up, boiling water for her coffee. "Good morning," I said.

"That's one thing in life you can count on," Tante Tina answered. "A good morning. After that, it's anybody's guess."

I followed her around, learning the routine. Inside the little barn, odours of straw and chicken manure mingled with the musty smell of old concrete. The gentle brown Jersey cow called Klempie blinked at me with her big brown cow eyes. Tante Tina had already milked her, and it would be my job to pour the bucket of fresh warm milk into a little tub above the cream separator where a filter strained out any bits of straw or dirt that got in. We set up the separator in the cool breezeway of the house. Tante Tina showed me how to crank the handle, which spun a funnel filled with thin metal membranes that magically directed the rich cream into the upper spout and the "blue milk" out the bottom into pitchers. While I cranked, she went to the chicken coop and made sure the hens had grain and water. When the milk was separated, we went back to the barn. I slid my hands beneath the hens' feathered breasts to retrieve their eggs. Then I washed the eggs in a pail of water and, when they were dry, tucked them into egg cartons.

Later we poured the thick cream into her butter churn and spent half an hour whipping the cream into butter. The fresh milk we poured into a big pot and heated slowly until it solidified into curds that we strained out and sold as *glomms*. We always saved some for our own use too.

After those chores, it was time for breakfast, my favourite meal of the day. We drank coffee together. I liked mine milky. Tina drank hers strong with fresh cream. She ate fresh sweet cream for breakfast, with a dollop of jam, scooping the mixture up with her twice-baked buns called *reeschtje*. I dunked the buns in my coffee, ate them with cheese and apricot jam. We ate until we were full, and it became our custom to sit in our chairs for a few minutes after breakfast and discuss the day's events.

"Today we pick the first strawberries," Tante Tina said. "And tonight we'll make jam. I like to pick in the cool of the morning, when the dew is still on the leaves. That way it's more fun." She winked at me. We took our plates to the sink, promising to wash them later, and headed to the garden.

The strawberries were hidden like treasures beneath cool wet leaves that tickled my ankles. We crawled along the rows, plucking the red berries and dropping them into green quart baskets. Above us, the sun rose into a clear blue sky. As the day heated up, the chirruping of robins and croaking of crows faded into silence and the cicadas in the ash and poplar trees that bordered Tante Tina's orchard began a shrill ringing that swelled and crescendoed and faded into silence, and then began again.

"Don't forget to eat some," Tante Tina reminded me. "That's the best part of picking!"

By midday, Mennonite housewives, proud of their cooking, who liked to use traditional ingredients, began to arrive. Tante Tina sold them Klempie's fresh milk and cream, homemade *glomms,* butter, eggs, and fresh fruit and vegetables in season. Others came to her with their aches and pains. Tante Tina always had time for her callers; this is how she accumulated her repertoire of stories.

"This one," Tante Tina rejoined me in the garden after her first customer departed, "was separated from her husband in Russia. See how sad and pinched she looks. Fifteen years later, when she was already here in Canada, she discovered that her man was still alive. He survived the work camp and the war and the *flucht,* but, thinking she was dead, he remarried and had four children with his new wife. This one never smiles."

"And that one," she pointed her chin at the disappearing hunchback of a man who came to her with his deformed shoulder later that morning, "he was supposed to be married, way back in Russia. Just before his wedding, his father-in-law-to-be sent him to the big town to get medicine for their horse. When he got back, the day before his wedding, his bride-to-be was dead, killed of blood poisoning. She'd stepped on a rusty nail in the barn, and in those days, if you did that, you were *kaput.* They buried her in her wedding dress. He's come for massage once a month for thirty years, never looked once at another woman."

About one feisty, white-haired lady, she shook her head and said, "She raised five children, by herself. Though she was married, her husband was more of a baby than any of them. He hated farm work. The smell of cow dung made him sick. All he wanted to do was write. Once, she told me, she went into the barn and discovered that instead of milking the cows, he was writing a poem in white chalk on the wooden walls of his cow barn. She had to milk the cows that morning and every morning after that. It turned out she liked the cow barn. And her husband spent mornings inside writing. At his funeral they read one of his poems."

Just after noon, we finished the first picking of the strawberry patch and headed to the house for lunch. Tante Tina wanted to make *kotletten,* some for us and some to take to a friend whose mother had died. I sat in the cool kitchen with Mietze the cat in my lap and watched Tante Tina mix up a batch of Mennonite meatballs, made with ground beef, salt and pepper, cornflakes, and an egg. She tested for seasoning by licking a bit of the raw meat mixture off her finger. Soon the house was filled with the mouth-watering smell of the meat sizzling in a heavy pan.

Someone knocked on the door. I jumped up, spilling Mietze onto the ground, to answer. It was a scrawny woman with an enormous amount of silvery black hair fastened to the top of her head with combs and bobby pins. She was old but vigorous. Tante Tina rolled her eyes at me before turning to greet her.

"Hello Gerda," my aunt said, drying her hands on her apron.

I went back to my chair and coaxed Mietze back onto my lap.

The old lady sniffed the air like a dog, and her face scrunched into a frown of distaste at the smell of the frying *kotletten*. She shook her head violently, back and forth, so that her bun wagged at the back of her head, and she brandished her forefinger as good as a preacher.

"Nah, Tinche," she admonished, "are you still eating that devil's meat?"

Tante Tina laughed, a snort out her nostrils, and flipped the burgers in their pan of sizzling fat. "No," she answered. "I've changed my ways. You're right. All this fat isn't good for us. No," she looked at Gerda. "I'm making these *kotletten* for Mietze and her kittens. You know how they love their meat. This is mouse meat that I ground up and spiced specially for the cats."

Gerda didn't know if Tante Tina was telling the truth, but she deflated like a sheet on the clothesline when the wind suddenly stops blowing. She bought some *glomms* and left quickly. My aunt and I laughed until, as she said in *Plautdietsch,* we had to bite our bellies.

As soon as we dried our eyes, Tante Tina put a huge cauldron of water to boil, then went to the henhouse and chose a plump chicken. She wrung its neck with a deft twist of her wrist and showed me how to dip it into hot water and pluck it. She saved the feathers for a winter quilt and began a pot of her famous chicken noodle soup. While the pot bubbled and steamed, we nibbled on *kotletten* and made noodles for the soup, nice fat strings of dough that we dipped into the broth at the very end. "Now look at this," she said, and slid her ladle under a ring of fat in the soup.

"There once was a Russian nobleman, very rich and dressed in furs, with drooping moustaches and a tall, woollen hat. He was riding through the colonies one day, and night fell before he reached his destination. He stopped at a farmhouse and asked the *Hausfrau* to make him a good, hearty soup. If she would make sure there were fat rings as big as gold coins floating on top, he would reward her with as many gold coins as there were fat rings. She set to work making a good soup, stuck a ham bone in the pot and let it cook. She went down to the cellar for some potatoes. When she was gone, her husband, a simple but greedy peasant, lifted the lid and saw only a few fat rings on top of the broth. The rich nobleman, seeing the greed in the farmer's eyes, muttered that he would be willing to give them as many as ten gold coins if there were that many fat rings. The farmer counted only three, and so he went to the shelf where his wife kept the pork lard, and added a generous scoop to the soup, intending to make them rich. When the soup was finished, there was so much fat in it that only one big round fat ring the size of the entire pot formed. The nobleman got his fatty soup, and didn't have to pay a thing for it, since the one fat ring was much bigger than any of his gold coins."

Tante Tina laughed when she finished the story. "I don't think that woman forgave her man until the day he thankfully died," she said, wiping her eyes with her apron.

Then there were plenty of dishes to wash. The day was turning toward evening, cooling after the heat of midday. The oaks around the house absorbed the setting sun and shaded us with syrupy light. No more visitors came, and we worked quietly to finish the day's chores. We washed and hulled the strawberries and boiled them up with sugar for jam. We ate the noodle soup for dinner. My arms were sore from cranking the milk separator, my skin tingled from the sun. My belly was sore from laughing so hard, and that part inside of me that was usually hard and angry was soft and happy.

We drained our soup bowls with slurps. "I couldn't do that if I was the queen of England," said Tante Tina. I smiled, too tired to even laugh. "I'll do the supper dishes," my aunt said to me. "Why don't you have a bath and go to bed."

It was all I could do to remove my clothes. I dropped them in a heap beside the bathtub, soaked for a few minutes, scrubbed off the ground-in dirt from the strawberry patch, dried myself quickly, and slid into my nightgown. I was in bed before it was dark. The light outside my window was grey and dusky, like newsprint, and I could hear the swish and hiss of wind in the oak leaves.

It had been a day of stories and people and work, and a warmth and peace that came from Tante Tina. I was too tired even to read. Anyway, this life was better than a book. I couldn't hear the foghorns because we were far from Lake Ontario. I didn't miss their mournful song.

THREE LITTLE KITTENS

The first week passed, each day slow and unhurried, but full and rich. There was always something to do and we were never in a hurry. It didn't seem possible that these days were the same length that days had always been. They seemed longer and much deeper.

I didn't want to go home that first weekend, I was so happy living with Tante Tina. But then I felt guilty about neglecting my parents and, when my father picked me up on Friday after work, I wanted to be extra nice to him.

On the way home, we stopped to buy groceries at Art Goossen Groceries. Shopping with my father was fun. The ladies in the delicatessen were friendly to my dad, and asked how I was. I said I was staying at my Tante Tina's house for the summer, that I was just home for the weekend, and then I asked for a half a pound of farmer's cheese so my dad and I could make our favourite sandwiches. They laughed, said I was a daddy's girl, and I smiled too.

In the parking lot my dad and I put our groceries in the car. A group of migrant workers climbed aboard their bicycles, balanced their boxes of groceries on the bar between their legs, and rode off home like that. They did things so differently from everybody else in Homer. They laughed out loud as they tried to balance the groceries on their bikes. One of them saw me watching and called out, "Hi!" I smiled and waved back, but my dad didn't like that.

I thought we'd go straight home, but my father gave me a bad surprise. He stopped at my grandfather's place. I wished I could just stay in the car, but I followed my dad. Opa's yard was wild with untrimmed grass, a maple tree with leaves as big as plates, and fat hydrangea blooms that dripped petals like snow. It was windy and I liked the feeling of the strong, warm breeze tugging at my hair. My dad went looking for my grandfather. I lagged behind, catching petals in my palms.

Opa was in the barn, his favourite place. He kept pigeons in a coop divided from the rest of the barn by chicken wire. The big purply-grey birds could fly in and out of the coop as they liked, and little groups of them sat in the rafters cooing and murmuring. I walked into the cool barn. I could hear the wind outside; inside the barn it was still. In the light of the slanting afternoon sun, dust motes spun in mid-air. I didn't even mind my grandfather in that moment; his barn was like a church.

Opa was a tall, stooped man, with long, straggly,

white hair that fringed his bald head. His ears were the size of small saucers and his shiny forehead flared red when he got angry, which was often. He was always in a bad mood, complaining of aches and pains, a sore back, gout, gas, and general stiffness. He lived alone now.

My Oma died when I was a little girl, but I remembered the German fairy tales she had told me.

I wasn't really sure what my grandfather did for work when he was a younger man. My dad said he'd done whatever he had to do to survive when they first came to Canada. He worked in the orchards, at the canning factory in St. David, and he helped other Mennonite farmers during pig slaughter time and with barn raising. He had a reputation for being a good sausage maker. He nursed my Oma until she died of cancer, and after that he became a hermit, confined by his own accord to his yard, where he kept a messy garden and a ragged orchard.

He lived on the edge of Homer, in a yard close to my creek, in one of the last remaining old farmhouses. It was crooked and wooden, tilted after a part of the basement caved in, covered on one side by black tarpaper, and accompanied by a rotting wooden barn that looked as if it was made of matchsticks. A good wind might blow it over. It was where my father had grown up, but it was not a place I liked to visit.

My Opa was a strange man, and bitter about life. He preferred the company of his many pigeons to people, and as a child I was terrified of him, didn't like his smell of barn and birds. Now he embarrassed me. I was afraid my friends would see him on his property, with feathers sticking out of his hat, his pants and boots spattered with pigeon droppings, carrying his birds on his forearms as he walked through his garden, singing to them and kissing them. He was sweet and gentle to the pigeons, but he was mean and nasty to everybody else.

When we arrived, Opa was inside the pigeon cage. He had a broom with him, but he wasn't sweeping the dirty hay from the floor. Instead, he was standing still, stroking a pigeon that sat on his wrist. I watched as he petted it, raised it to his face and kissed it. He seemed kindly enough, but when he saw us his face changed. "I'm busy," he barked at my father in *Plautdietsch*. "Your hair looks like a haystack," he shot at me.

I didn't say anything, but stayed close to my dad. My father was gentle with him, inquiring about his health and asking him if he'd eaten that day. Opa listed his aches and pains and complained that he couldn't digest anything, so why bother eating.

He turned to my father then, shooing the pigeon off his wrist, and said he needed some help. He thrust a burlap sack into my father's hands and ordered him to go up into the hayloft and fetch the kittens that the neighbour's cat had birthed yesterday. "I can hear them up there," he said hoarsely in Low German. "They can't stay here because they'll eat my pigeons."

My father climbed up the ladder into the loft and

came back soon with a sackful of kittens who mewed loudly. The mother cat, skinny and wide-eyed, ran behind my father, her tail flicking high, her whiskers erect, mewing in concern. I watched, horrified, as Opa lifted his leg and kicked the mother cat, sending her flying out the barn door. Then he grabbed the bag from my dad and added a brick that he picked up from a pile beside the barn door. He twisted a knot into the neck of the sack, and with a quick motion, dropped the kittens into a rusty barrel of rainwater below the eavestrough spout.

Their mewing ceased instantly as the bag submerged, gurgling. I could hear the mother calling from the maple tree. Opa turned on his heel and re-entered the pigeon coop. He picked up the broom and told my dad to come in too, handed him a shovel and indicated that he should muck out the floor of the coop.

My father stood still for a moment beside the rain barrel. "It's not even his cat," I whispered, horrified and scared.

My dad wouldn't look at me. He meekly followed his father's instructions, turning to walk into the coop, reminding me of Daniel in the lion's den. I didn't say anything, but climbed quietly up the ladder to the hayloft. I couldn't believe what I had witnessed.

I found the spot where the mother cat had made her nest. The hay was tamped down in a circle, still warm when I touched my fingers to it. I looked around, thinking I was going to cry, and from a dark corner behind a bale of hay, I heard the sound of a hungry kitten. My father had missed one. I reached into the shadows and found the tiny, crying thing. It was still blind and nearly bald, trembling and calling for its mother. Its ears were laid flat against its head, and its head and neck stuck out like a turtle as it searched anxiously for the warmth and security of its siblings and mother.

From down below I heard the swish and scrape of the two men working in silence. The kitten began to mew as it discovered me. I was afraid my grandfather would hear, so I took off my shoe and threw it at the pigeons in the rafters hoping they'd make noise. They made a ruckus, squawking indignantly, flapping and scrabbling to find another place to roost, then settled down to cooing and chirping again. I took the little kitten by the scruff of her neck, held her close to quiet her, but she continued to mewl and cry.

In the next pause I heard my father say he would get hay from the loft, and he climbed up the rickety wooden steps to where I sat in the far corner, by the window thick with dust and cobwebs. The smell of dry grass and sweet clover was in my nose and I held the tiny creature in my hand. The kitten was quieter now, calmed by the warmth of my body. My father hefted a bale of hay and dropped it to the floor below. In the dust that erupted like a fountain around the bale, I sneezed and the kitten, startled, mewled again. My father hesitated on his way down the ladder. With only his head and shoulders in the loft, he looked for me, found me sitting in the corner.

I pleaded silently with him, held the tiny thing to my mouth, breathing on it to soothe it. My dad didn't say anything, just continued down the ladder. Then I heard him breaking apart the hay bale and spreading it onto the newly cleaned concrete floor of the pigeon coop. As he worked, he began to sing. He had a fine, strong tenor voice. I liked to hear him sing hymns at church, his tenor giving harmony to the voices of the other Mennonites who loved to sing.

It was one of my favourite songs. "When peace like a river attendeth my way," he sang. "When sorrows like sea billows roll." Opa said something in Low German, but my father continued. "Whatever my lot, thou hast taught me to say, it is well, it is well with my soul."

Then came the chorus. In church, with the full congregation singing all four parts, the chorus was like a great ocean swell, with the women starting and the men coming in afterward while the women sustained a high note and the men deepened the harmony. Then the women curled the wave above and the men brought it crashing down.

Singing solo, in the pigeon coop, my father's voice easily drowned the kitten's cries and my own whimpering, as I sobbed at my grandfather's cruelty and the helplessness of the animals.

When the chorus was finished, my father swept the dirty hay out the barn door and took Opa, protesting gutturally, along with him. I breathed again, relieved. The kitten was quiet. I scrambled out of the hayloft, straw caught in my clothes and my hair, the tiny kitten clutched to my chest. I checked to see if the coast was clear and made a dash for the edge of the property, not sure what to do with the little, blind thing. I ran to the back of the garden, where the tall green corn sheltered me from sight, and sank onto the ground in the middle of a weedy row.

The corn was just developing silken tassels and the wind tossed them like flags. I didn't feel like celebrating. One kitten was safe, but I didn't want to think about the others in the rain barrel. I sat on the earth, the warm kitten against my cheek. Its heart beat a tattoo against my skin, and I hummed the song my father had been singing.

"It is well, it is well, with my soul, with my soul. It is well, it is well, with my soul." I repeated the chorus and felt calmer and calmer, as though I was floating on an ocean swell, letting it lift me and catching me as I fell.

Then I heard a rustling in the tall grass between the corn rows. The mother cat appeared, her eyes wide and her mouth anxiously forming mewling calls. The kitten responded immediately, and I gently placed it in the soft, green summer grass. With one quick motion, as quickly as my grandfather had tied the knot, the mother cat sank her teeth into her baby's neck and snatched it up. Without a backward glance, she ran in the opposite direction from the barn and the rain barrel. As soon as she had the baby in her jaws, it stopped crying. The mother cat knew exactly what to do.

I watched her as she ran, tail up, away from my Opa, and I vowed, someday, to do the same.

I waited in the corn until my father called for me. We didn't say much on the way home. I tried to pretend that my grandfather wasn't related to me, but I was too old for this kind of fantasy. The silence in the car was sad. Did my dad feel sorry that I had seen the drowning? And that it was his father who had done it?

"You've got such a good voice," I said as I opened the door and let myself out. "Thank you for singing that song. It's my favourite hymn."

He nodded, and parked the car carefully in our garage. Inside the house, Chris was crying. Mary Anne held her against her chest, gently thumping her back to relieve some gas. My mother was at the stove, making gravy for supper. My father brought the groceries inside. Everything seemed normal, but I was scared for Chris. What if someone wanted to hurt her? It would be so easy.

Mary Anne just rocked Chris, patting her and soothing her with nonsense words. She didn't seem afraid.

"I can't eat anything," I said to my mother. "All that pigeon poop made me sick. I'll be back later."

I ran down the road to the creek, and climbed into my favourite willow tree. I wanted to feel like I was in a gently rocking sea, a place where I was safe.

SHELTER

On Monday morning my father drove me to Tante Tina's on his way to work. It was early, before six, and the sun was just coming over the horizon, a round, red fireball promising a long, hot day. We talked a little. I told him how the mother cat had found her kitten. He said the mothering instinct was strong.

"Your mother changed after she had you girls," he said to me. "She wasn't the girl I married any more."

"Mary Anne too," I said.

My father nodded. "I guess so," he said reluctanty.

He turned into Tante Tina's yard. She was up, giving the chickens water. She wore her housecoat and her hair covered her shoulders like a silver shawl. I knew she had the coffee started inside with a little pan of milk warming up on the next burner for me. She looked up at the car, smiled when she saw us, and I felt a flood of pleasant relief. The whole week stretched ahead.

She invited my dad for coffee and we went inside,

to sit and drink our coffee in the breezeway. I helped her pour three cups. *"Kaffee Tante,"* she teased me, and pinched my cheek between her thumb and forefinger. I thought of how the mother cat held her baby, so strong between her jaws. The baby went limp there, paralyzed and safe. Mietze meowed and Tante Tina let her into the house. She jumped onto my lap and purred while we drank our coffee. Tina offered my dad some *piroshke,* freshly baked on the weekend. He picked up the bun, bit into it, and smiled at the taste of the seasoned meat hidden inside.

"You are the best cook in the world," my dad said to her.

She smiled deeply, dimples appearing in her cheeks like a nice crease in bun dough.

"You just say that so I give you treats every Monday," she said to him. Then she added, "Well, I guess that's only fair, because you bring me such a nice treat too."

I smiled as I sipped my milky coffee. How could she be my Opa's sister, I wondered.

My father swallowed his last bite and drained his coffee. "Heigh ho, heigh ho," he sang, "it's off to work I go."

I didn't know he knew the dwarves' song. "Where did you learn that?" I asked him.

"From you," he said. "You were always singing something when you were a little girl."

I pictured the dwarves shouldering their shovels

and pickaxes, singing and whistling as they marched off to work. "What do the dwarves in the fairy tale do for work, anyway?" I pondered aloud.

"They toil and sweat for their daily bread," answered my father. "That's what we all do." He sounded glum.

"I'll trade you," I said. "Today you can work for Tante Tina and I'll report to the General."

Tante Tina laughed in the middle of her *schlucks* of coffee. She started choking and coughing so hard we had to bang her on the back. Even when the coughing stopped, she leaned back in her chair and laughed, shaking her head, and wiping her eyes with the bottom of her apron.

"You don't think I'd do as good a job as Tina?" my dad asked, his eyes twinkling. Tante Tina's laughter was infectious.

Tante Tina sobered up. "You I could work with. I was just picturing the General's reaction to Tina. Wouldn't his eyes bulge out at the sight of this little girl coming to do your work!"

Then my father laughed too, almost as hard as Tante Tina. "I could do it," I insisted. "You say the robots help with all the heavy work. I could press all the right buttons."

That sobered my dad up. "It's true," he said to Tante Tina. "One day they'll hire children to do the work, pay them less, and I won't have a job."

"It's more than just pushing buttons," Tante Tina reminded my dad. "You have to have the strength to stand still, to do the same job over and over again, without becoming discouraged. That takes a man."

"Maybe we could just get the dwarves to do the job," I said. "Then you could stay here with us. Never a dull moment!" I looked at Tante Tina. She winked at me with a nice smile.

"*Nah ja,*" said my dad. "It's been fun. But the General doesn't abide a tardy man." He brought his coffee cup to the counter beside the sink. "You be a good girl, Tina."

"You know I am, Dad." I hugged him and he drove to work, leaving me with Tante Tina and the whole week ahead.

Working with Tante Tina wasn't like work at all. We talked all the time and took enough breaks so I never got bored. If we were working in the orchard, we always kept our eyes open for robin's nests and watched the clouds changing in the sky. Tante Tina left the grass and weeds growing between the rows and called the weeds by their flower names – Queen Anne's Lace, cornflowers, buttercups.

Unlike most farmers, who picked their fruit unripe and hard so it could withstand transportation, Tante Tina picked her fruit when it was ripe. As soon as it came off the tree, she sold it or used it. People came from all around to buy her fruit because she didn't spray. All the other farmers used spray to kill insects, and to help the fruit ripen on time, or to colour up properly, or to prevent molds from growing, and to keep the fruit from bruising.

More than once I'd been caught in a fountain of spray as I cycled or walked past the orchards that started at the far end of Homer and continued up to the escarpment and down to the lake. The spray was cool when it touched the bare skin of my arms or my cheeks, and dried instantly. It smelled sour and tasted bitter and gave me goosebumps when it landed on me.

My uncle Bruno, Lorraine's father, sprayed his fruit trees and, when I asked him why, he said that's how it had to be done, or else the fruit would be too small, or wormy, or not the right colour. When Anna's father sprayed their orchard, he made sure the children were out of the way, and he tied a handkerchief around his face.

I worried about the migrant workers who spent the whole summer in the orchard without any protection. Nobody told them to get out of the way when the sprayer went by. Nobody took care of them at all.

But even without spray, Tante Tina's strawberries were plump and red, her cherries scarlet globes, the apricots orange and sweet, the peaches juicy. People said her fruit tasted better than the fruit they bought at the store.

"That's how it is when you let nature be," she told me. "And now you know the secret."

Birds ate some of her fruit, but she didn't complain. "That's life," she said. "We should all be able to find our food as easily."

It was a joy to go into the orchard in the cool of the morning, to pick the dewy fruit, without the threat of the bitter yellow powder getting into my hair and eyes.

On our first July morning in the cherry orchard, I said to Tante Tina, "Some Mennonite farmers say that people who don't spray their orchards are bad for the other farms. Their fruit attracts bugs and birds who forget they're not supposed to eat the other farmers' fruit."

Tante Tina looked into her basket. It was half-full of sour cherries. They were too tart to eat off the tree, better cooked with sugar for jam and pie fillings, but I popped a few fresh ones into my mouth and started salivating. She sorted through the cherries in her basket with her juice-stained fingers, pulled some leaves and twigs out without saying anything.

"And," I continued, "last winter Anna and I were playing in their barn. We found a bag of yellow powder that they dump into the peach wash when they're packing peaches. There was a big warning on the bag. The label said it could cause cancer. It doesn't seem right, to use the yellow powder that might cause cancer, and then eat the peaches. Before I saw the bag, I just fished a peach out of the wash and ate it right there. I thought it was clean!"

Tante Tina sighed and set her basket on the ground. She removed her harness and told me to do the same. Then she rinsed her hands with water she had brought along and poured us each some iced tea. She sat on the ground under a cherry tree and motioned for me to sit down. We sat under the old cherry tree, back to back with the gnarled trunk between our spines. The sun was hot, but the leaves filtered it, cooled it, and patterned us with leaf shadows. We sipped until the jar of iced tea was empty.

"Do you think I'll get cancer from that yellow powder?" I asked my aunt. "I don't want to get cancer," I added. "Cancer gives you tumours all over your body, and it hurts."

"Nah, Miale," she started. "When I was a girl I didn't once think about such things. Death was for old people. And here I am. Still alive. And you too."

"Well, what if...." I insisted.

"If you got cancer, you might die," Tante Tina said bluntly. "Or you might get better and live for a long time. Like me."

"You had cancer?" I asked her, horrified.

"Yes, but it's gone now."

"But it might come back!"

"Maybe. Maybe not."

Tante Tina was so calm. I was shivering with fear. "I don't want you to die," I insisted.

"I am going to die," she said calmly. "Some day. And so are you. And at that moment of death, it won't matter if it was cancer or a heart attack or old age or an accident. It will only matter that you lived

112

your life like you weren't afraid to die, *ja?*"

I couldn't answer.

"If the doctor told me today that I had two weeks left to live, I wouldn't change anything." She winked at me. "I'd just live every day like I'm living them now. Milking Klempie in the morning, drinking coffee with her nice fresh cream. Eating a handful of ripe fruit when I need a snack. Talking with you. Laughing all the time."

As she talked, I began to feel a bit better. Sitting right here, with my bum on the ground and my bare heels pressing into baked earth, the taste of iced tea in my mouth, my fingers sticky from picking fruit.

"I feel safe now, because I'm with you and you're not scared," I said. "But sometimes when I go to bed at night I close my eyes and I see that bag of yellow powder with the big warning – cancer."

I stopped talking because I could see that Tante Tina was fuming. I thought she was mad at me, and I didn't know why.

Finally Tante Tina spoke.

"See this ground," she said, digging up a handful and sifting it through her splayed fingers. Some of the dirt trickled onto my leg and it tickled me. "If we could eat this, life would be a lot simpler."

I laughed.

"But we can't," she said. "So we have to remember that this earth is our mother. It feeds us and nourishes us, protects us, and receives us."

"In the Bible it says God made Adam from the

earth," I said. "But not Eve. Why does she come from Adam's rib and not from the earth?"

"You can forget that nonsense," Tante Tina snorted. "Woman comes from the earth too. And you can be sure that we all return to the earth in the end."

"It'll take a long time," I said remembering my Oma's funeral, the thick wooden coffin, the cement-lined grave, the preservative in her veins that made her look younger than when she was alive.

"Yes, and maybe all the chemicals the farmers spray on their fruit will make it take even longer. Maybe that's why they do it. Maybe they're afraid to die, and they want to be preserved forever.

"Oh," I answered, "they're not afraid to die. They know they're going to heaven!"

Tante Tina snorted. "Maybe they're not so sure!"

I made a face. "It doesn't make sense, though. If they're all Christians, shouldn't they care about their workers? Their families? About the people who eat their fruit? Some of it goes all the way to Montreal! And what about the bugs that die and the birds that get sick from eating them?"

I often found dead birds in the willows beside the creek, soft robin's eggs that didn't have birds inside, and bloated carp with tumours floating belly up in the creek. In explorations up the creek, I'd found big metal drums half submerged. The farmers discarded the containers their sprays came in and left them to rust in the creek. I guess they didn't think of the creek as much more than a dump. That made me angry too.

"Why doesn't it say somewhere in the Bible that we have to take care of the earth and treat it well, if it's so important?" I asked Tante Tina.

"Well, the Bible was written a long time ago and translated by many people who wanted their message to be told! It misses a lot of important information," she said. "You really can't count on it to tell you what to do. It's more important to know what *you* think is right for you."

She emphasized her words with her finger and pushed me backward onto the ground. I didn't mind. I pressed my back into the sun-hot soil. Heat radiated into my skin and up and down my spine. I felt dreamy.

I let myself think about death, about being dead. I knew that I was going to die, someday, and that dying probably wouldn't be fun. I considered what it would feel like to feel nothing. I pretended to be dead, to be nothing. But the more I felt the heat in my body and the wind on my skin, the less I could think about death. And the more I thought about fried potatoes and sausages for dinner, the more alive I felt. And the longer I stayed with Tante Tina, the happier I became about being alive. Each day was full of mystery and adventures, even if it was just learning how to make butter or discovering a new channel in the creek.

Tante Tina sat quietly beside me. The wind whispered in my ears and ruffled my hair. I thought it was running fingers through my hair, but when I opened my eyes, I saw that Tante Tina was smiling at me and stroking my head.

"I love summer," she said.

"Me too."

"And fresh peas from the garden."

"Mm-hmm."

"A baby's soft head."

"Reading a book in a willow tree."

"When all the company leaves and you're home alone again."

"Breakfast!"

"Lunch and dinner!"

"Being here with you!"

"Having you here with me."

"Kittens."

"Making bread."

"Eating it!"

"Eating period."

"Eating dirt."

Tante Tina got serious. "On my farm you could eat the earth if you liked the flavour."

I smiled lazily.

"I'd rather eat your *platz*," I said. "With cherries in it, and coffee."

"Nah ja," she answered. "It's getting too hot to pick. Let's go home. It must be time for lunch."

We left our ladders beneath the trees, to be collected later, and each carried a basket of cherries back to the barn. The sun was high in the sky. Crickets chirped and cicadas buzzed like motors. I felt the muscles in my arm working.

"I think all the bugs come to your place," I said. "Because they know it's safe."

She nodded.

"Just like me," I added.

"You're no bug!" she said. Then added, "Well, maybe sometimes!"

I didn't mind because she winked at me when she said it and squeezed my shoulder with her free hand.

KOLYA

On Friday afternoon of that week, Tante Tina and I were in the barn packing cherries, sorting through them to remove the rotten and unripe ones and picking out bits of leaves and stems, when we heard a car drive onto the driveway and stop on the other side of the bridge.

"The day has flown by!" exclaimed Tante Tina, thinking it was my dad come to pick me up. But it was Mary Anne, wearing a pretty yellow dress and white sandals, carrying Chris in her little car seat.

She walked toward us. I called out, telling her to come to the barn. She set Chris down on the packing table and smiled at us. I hadn't looked at her carefully lately. She looked pretty, a little older, a little rounder, and very happy. Her dark red hair was curly and she tucked it behind her ears.

"So, who are we? Special people you have to dress up for!" Tante Tina had her face close to Chris, but she was speaking to Mary Anne.

"Dad came home early today," Mary Anne said.

"The General sent some men home because they didn't need everybody now that the robots help them do the work. Dad was very worried. He says that some of the men will lose their jobs. I just had to get out of the house."

"Well, you've come to the right spot, my girl," said Tante Tina. "That's enough for today, Tina," she said to me. "Let's get washed up and have a good visit! I've got an idea for supper!"

She strode toward the house with big wide steps, leaving Mary Anne and me far behind.

"Are you having fun, Tina?" my sister asked me.

"Yes," I said immediately and forcefully.

Mary Anne smiled. "Good," she said.

"Are you?" I asked her.

She nodded. "I'm happy to take care of Chris," she answered. "But Mom and Dad...."

I couldn't understand how Mary Anne could like taking care of Chris all day and all night, every day, day after day, with no time to herself, no freedom to run to the creek with a book whenever she wanted to. But as I thought about it, I realized she'd never done that, even when she didn't have Chris. I thought that I didn't really understand my sister, and that maybe I could never really understand anyone who wasn't me.

Tante Tina stuck her head out the kitchen door. "Why don't you girls sit in the swing and have a good talk. I'm going to be busy in the kitchen for a minute or two."

"Don't you need some help?" I called back.

"When I do, I'll call you."

At first Mary Anne and I sat quietly, swinging gently. Chris slept in her chair beside us, and Mary Anne seemed happy that Chris was quiet.

Then Mary Anne started talking. "Mom and Dad aren't getting along so well," she said.

"Why not?" I asked, feeling a pit of fear begin to open in my stomach.

"Well, Mom doesn't go to church anymore. That might not be so bad, except she tells Dad what she thinks about all the people there, the way they do things. She's mad that they don't like me and Chris."

"Who wouldn't like Chris?" I said, looking at her sleeping face. "As if she did anything wrong!"

"That's what Mom says. She says that the church people should use their brains instead of their Bibles all the time. Dad doesn't like that."

"Maybe he's afraid she's going to sin against the Holy Spirit by saying those things," I said. No one could say exactly what you had to do to sin against the Holy Spirit, but if you did it, you could never, in a million forevers, be forgiven. That worried me at night.

"I don't know," said Mary Anne, in a voice that really said, I don't care.

It was that perfect time of afternoon, the time I looked forward to all day, when the sun was halfway down the other side of the sky and seemed to slowly melt, turn egg yolk yellow, and dissolve into golden syrup. The oak leaves above our heads formed a breezy canopy. Chris stirred in her sleep, but only enough to stretch and open her mouth like a kitten, then rearrange herself into a cozy curl of baby and sleep.

I was jealous of how comfortable she was. I wished I could sleep like that, pure and uncomplicated by feelings of fear and anxiety. But there were so many questions that had no answers, and so many fears that made me fret. In particular, I'd started remembering something about my Opa, something that made me feel horrible and dirty, something that made me angry, something that a little girl like Chris should, and would, never know.

My thoughts were interrupted by two things – I noticed that Mary Anne had fallen asleep in the swing, and I smelled the delicious aroma of carrots and onions, and something roasting from inside the kitchen. I got up out of the swing quietly and walked carefully to Tante Tina's kitchen doorway without disturbing Chris and Mary Anne.

Tante Tina was at the stove. She'd had a bath and her hair was wet. It was held up by only one silver comb. Little drops of water trailed down her neck and disappeared into her blouse down her back. She was wearing an apron and stirring a steaming pot. I could smell onions, parsley, and bay leaf. On the counter beside the stove was a pyramid of potato pieces. As I watched, she dropped handfuls into the steaming broth. I didn't think she'd heard me come in, but as I stood there, she addressed me. "This soup needs a bit of dill. Why don't you find some in the garden."

I moved toward her quickly, overwhelmed by the urge to hug her solid body. When I put my arms around her, she patted my forearms with her cool, wet hands.

"What's that for?" she asked.

"For being so nice. For being Tante Tina. For having me here!"

"Oh, that," she laughed. "That's nothing. That's easy."

She patted my hands again, then shooed me out to the garden.

I tiptoed past Mary Anne, shaded and cool in the swing, and found a patch of tangy summer dill, tall and curved like lacy green umbrellas. I picked a couple of stalks and held them to my nose. Pickles came to mind, crunchy, tasty dill pickles eaten with fresh buns and cheese. Suddenly I felt hungry and ran back to the kitchen with the herbs.

Mary Anne was sitting at the kitchen table, feeding Chris. Tante Tina took the dill and pulled it apart and dropped it into the steaming pot. "Can you guess what I'm making?" she asked me. "It's your favourite." Tante Tina winked at Mary Anne.

My sister laughed. "Everything's her favourite!" That was the family joke.

"That's right," said Tante Tina. Then she said to me, "Why don't you have a cool bath and change into something pretty. I feel like celebrating, making this a special evening. It's not every night that it's just us ladies!"

I didn't have a good dress along – the only time I wore dresses was to go to church, and I certainly didn't do that at Tante Tina's – but I had a bath and washed my hair and combed it so that it would dry neatly. My hair was getting longer. It hung down around my collarbones and I thought it looked nice at this length. I put on a clean pair of green shorts and my best shirt – a white blouse with little pink and green flowers – and then I went downstairs. Tante Tina smiled approvingly and tucked a loose strand of hair behind my ears.

She'd changed too, while I was bathing, but it wasn't her dress that made me gasp – it was pretty enough, black with lace around the collar and cuffs and a brooch at her throat – it was her hair. She never wore it down, except to sleep. It was long and wavy, hanging almost down to her waist, held back from her face with two bright combs. The silvery hair against the black of her dress was stunning, and I knew she was more beautiful than me or Mary Anne, even though we were young and she was old.

She made me think of an empress. I curtsied and said, "My lady," and took her hand in mine.

It was strong and warm, with long muscular fingers, lined all over from her hard work. I wondered if I would ever be as beautiful as she was.

"Nah ja," said Tante Tina. "I guess this is just

dressing up. If I was such a fine lady, I would have a servant!"

"You can give me orders," I told her smiling. "You usually do!"

"Well," she said. "Let's pretend we're rich enough to give the poor servant girl a day off her chores."

Mary Anne smiled, looking like a sunflower in her yellow dress. She held Chris to her chest and rubbed her back to get a burp out. I helped Tante Tina bring food to the table.

Dinner was *butter suppe,* a creamy, buttery potato soup with melt-in-your-mouth carrots, chewy little dumplings, and a dab of sour cream in the oniony broth. It really was my favourite.

Tante Tina had spread the table with her good tablecloth, the one with hand-embroidered roses around the edges and a big rose in the middle.

Pretending to be a fine, rich lady made me eat slowly. I sipped the soup from the spoon into my mouth and let the soup rest on my tongue before swallowing.

"Tante Tina," I said. "Tell us a story." Mary Anne had placed Chris in her chair, and served herself some soup.

She looked at Tante Tina with an expectant smile.

Tante Tina thought for a moment, finished her bowl of soup, and sat back in her chair. "Well," she began. "You calling me a fine lady reminds me of a time when I dreamed of being one."

I knew better than to interrupt. I offered another

ladleful of *butter suppe* to Mary Anne.

"It was the closest I ever came to being a fine lady! We lived on a farm," continued Tante Tina. "It was a hard year. There was famine in the Ukraine. Crop failures, skirmishes, gangs of soldiers on horseback – we didn't know who was good, the Reds or the Whites, and there were threats of war. My mother grew a garden, so we had enough food for the summer. But we had to work hard. Many fields were empty, nobody grew grain. It was too dry and the grass didn't grow either. We only had one cow and she was skinny. Her calf died in the spring. That meant we had very little milk, so we didn't have much butter. Only enough to make *zwieback* on Saturdays. We ate plain, dark bread the rest of the week. I was about your age, Tina. I hated all the hard work. I hated milking the cow, I hated churning the butter, and I hated hoeing the beets. I was a dreamer, always wishing for a nice dress and a big meal with cream."

I interrupted the story to ask for more *butter suppe* and everyone laughed.

"One day in late summer, my mother scraped the bottom of the flour barrel," Tante Tina continued. "We'd slaughtered the last pig because we didn't have enough scraps to keep him fat."

"Were you scared?" Mary Anne asked.

"Well, there were potatoes in the garden. They weren't ready yet, but there were plenty of them. And carrots too. I was only a child, even though I was sixteen," Tina said winking at me. "My parents always took care of the problems. Anyway," she paused, "I was in love."

"What? You never told me!" I nearly shouted, my spoonful of soup forgotten halfway to my mouth.

Tante Tina gathered her fingers beneath her chin. She looked mysterious. I forgot about my soup.

"He was the doctor's son, a rich boy who loved the Mennonite farms because he secretly wanted to be a veterinarian. His father always brought him along on house calls to make a gentleman doctor out of him. But Kolya was happy to come along to visit the animals."

"Kolya," said Mary Anne. "Is that a Russian name?"

"It's short for Nikolai," said Tante Tina.

"What did he look like?" I asked.

"He was tall and slim, and he always wore a hat. A real gentleman. He was sad when our calf died, but he said nothing could be done. One morning my mother sent me to the summer pasture to get the cow. She wanted to see if the cow was fattening up. As I walked along the road, I saw the doctor's carriage up ahead. It passed me. Kolya and his father lifted their hats as they went by. I was thrilled. I pretended I was a real lady and that Kolya wanted to marry me. I didn't even hear the carriage come back a few minutes later.

"Kolya stopped beside me and said he had an hour before he had to pick up his father. He invited me into his carriage."

"Ooh," I squealed, and looked at Mary Anne. Her

eyes were bright. "Did you do it?" I asked breathlessly.

"Of course," said Tante Tina. "We only had a rough farm cart. I wanted to ride in his fine carriage. He was so different from the Mennonites. He had a moustache and sideburns and his mother's maid always starched his collar and cuffs. He said they choked him, and in the carriage he undid the buttons. We went down to the river."

Tante Tina had a private spot too!

"He said he would catch me a fish, but I didn't believe him. No rod, no net, and him in his good clothes. I laughed. He said he'd show me, and called me *Tinche Marie.*"

"I didn't know you had a middle name!"

"You don't know everything, *Miale!* There's always something to learn."

"And then what happened?" Mary Anne was curious.

"He tied his horse to an oak tree beside the river, took off his jacket and rolled up his sleeves. He wore suspenders with silver clips over his white shirt. And around his upper arms he wore black elastics to keep his shirt neat. He was as clean as a freshly made bed. Then he took off his socks and boots and rolled up his pant legs."

"Ooh," I squealed.

"He took me by the hand and told me to sit on a rock and watch. So I did. My hand was tingling and I forgot that my mama was waiting for me to bring the cow back from the summer pasture to see if she had any milk in her. I just sat there and watched Kolya. He was so gentle. He had a way with animals, it was his gift. It was too bad his father didn't understand. Kolya found a quiet shaded spot on the river. He leaned over and stuck a hand in the water up to his wrist. Then he wiggled his fingers and whistled a tune. He waited and I watched. My heart was tingling. I didn't say a word, only listened to his song and to my heart. I heard some splashing, then it was quiet again. Very patiently we all waited. Then boom! He plunged both arms into the water and flipped them up quickly, so fast that he splashed me and sent a big fish flying toward me. I screamed and ran out of the way. He told me to catch it, and the two of us chased that fish along the bank as it bucked and twisted trying to get back in the water. Finally it tired, lay gasping on the ground. Kolya got a rock and hit its head, then he looked up at me and said it was for me."

"Nice present," I giggled. "A dead fish."

"When you're starving," said Mary Anne, "it is a nice present!"

"Oh, yes," agreed Tante Tina. "I knew just what to do. I took the fish and wrapped it in some long grasses from the river's edge. While I did that, Kolya took off his shirt to shake out the creases."

"Did he have a muscular chest?" I asked.

"I didn't look," said Tante Tina. "We were too shy in those days. He got dressed, pulled his black wool jacket over his wet shirt, laced up his boots, and rolled down his pants. If you didn't look too close, he looked pretty clean. When it was time to get into the carriage, he took my hand like I was a real lady. I held my skirts and climbed up. Then he placed the fish in my lap and bowed. We both laughed. He jumped aboard and slapped the reins against the horse's rump."

"So, was your mother mad?" I asked.

"Nah ja," continued Tina, "my mother was good and mad at me. The cow was bawling when I brought her home. She had waited too long to be milked. And my father hated fish. He said it smelled rotten and he didn't like it cooked in the house. So my mother made a fire in the outside oven and, after stuffing the fish with onions and cracked wheat and parsley, we barbecued it."

"Yum," I said.

"But what about Kolya?" asked Mary Anne.

"Well, I never heard if his mother was upset about his wet shirt. You see, that day he told his father he wanted to be a veterinarian, and his father got so angry he sent him to Moscow to study to become a doctor."

"Parents!" I said, and Mary Anne nodded.

"And then the war came along," said my aunt. "By that time he was already a doctor, and he went to the front. His parents didn't want him to go, but by then he was too old to take orders. In the fighting he was killed and I never saw him again."

"I'll bet his parents were sorry then," I said. "If they'd let him become a vet, he would have been safe at home."

"It's a funny thing that life doesn't usually go the way you think," said Tante Tina. *"Miale,"* she exclaimed, startling me. "Your soup's gone cold!"

Listening to Tante Tina's story I'd forgotten all about my dinner. "That's okay," I said, "I'm saving room for dessert!"

"How did you know, *Miale?"*

"You always make dessert, especially for special occasions."

Tante Tina smiled. Mary Anne and I cleared the dishes away while my aunt made coffee. She poured three mugs full of steaming black liquid and carried the cake to the table. It was not fancy, decorated simply with roasted oats. It was something new.

"This is the cake my mother made the day after I brought the fish home. Even though my mother was mad at me, she made me a poor man's *Napoleon's torte* to thank me for bringing home the fish."

Tante Tina served us each a piece. It was layered, alternating light and dark, and sweet and soft. I ate my piece quickly.

But Mary Anne was slower. While she nibbled she examined the cake, broke bits off and looked at it closely.

"Do you know what it is?" asked Tante Tina.

"Well, it's not really cake," guessed Mary Anne. "Bread?"

"Worse," laughed Tante Tina. "Stale bread! Leftover! What else?"

"Something creamy that's not cream," said my sister.

"Cottage cheese," said my aunt.

"Bread and cottage cheese!" I stopped chewing for a minute. "Well, it tastes good anyway."

"No eggs, no flour, no butter, just a bit of sugar, some milk, and dried bread."

"I guess I can have two pieces then," I said, holding out my plate. "It's not fattening and it's just leftovers."

Tante Tina served me a second. "Do you like the coffee?" she asked.

"It's different," said Mary Anne. "It tastes burnt. Like charcoal," she giggled. "I don't mean to be impolite."

"I don't mind," Tante Tina said. "It's not impolite if it's true."

Mary Anne nodded.

"It's made from leftover bread too," said Tante Tina. "Toasted until it's black, then crumbled. Just the thing for three fine ladies! It's what we drank during the hard years. *Pripps* we called it."

"To *pripps*," I giggled. We all raised our cups in a toast.

We took our drinks outside onto the swing, Mary Anne carrying Chris in her chair. The evening air was fresh after the hot summer day. I could smell drying grass and the sweet smell of clover in the air. Summer was just settling in. I felt safe and loved with my aunt, my sister, and my niece all sitting beside and around me. My legs beneath the green shorts were cool, but it felt good,

131

because I knew tomorrow would be another hot day.

"Cozy as four bugs in a rug," said Tante Tina, sipping her coffee.

We couldn't really swing, because we were all on one side. I thought about Tante Tina as a girl my age. Fifteen was a good age. I knew a lot of things, but when I thought of Tante Tina now, I saw there was still a lot to learn. She had been a teenager like me, with dreams of romance, and look what had happened! The war, the soldiers, her brother, her girls. She wouldn't have guessed in a million years that all those things would happen to her.

"Were you disappointed about how your life turned out?" I asked her. "I mean, you had a crush on Kolya and you never saw him again."

Tante Tina sipped. Mary Anne and I stared up at the sky. The sun had set and the sky was deep orange and a moon was trying to shine through a fine layer of clouds on the horizon. We couldn't see stars yet. A breeze touched my warm cheeks.

When Tante Tina spoke, I had almost forgotten my question.

"Nah ja," she said. "Why shouldn't my mother be angry at me for forgetting about the cow? There was a famine and we were desperate. I was sorry to see Kolya go to Moscow, but I didn't really think we could ever be together. There was too much that kept us apart. Life was too busy to feel sorry for myself. My dreams helped me finish the work I had

to do. Actually," she continued, "I've found life to be better than my dreams for it. And it just keeps getting better."

Chris woke up then, and she started fussing. Mary Anne went inside to change her diaper, and Tante Tina followed. I sat in the swing and pictured Tante Tina, just a little older than I was now. I thought about turning sixteen. Was I ready to fall in love? I didn't think so. But I was learning to churn butter and to milk Klempie, and Tante Tina and I were having good discussions. One step at a time, I thought, that's the way to grow up.

DANCING

That weekend my mom asked me to come with
her to a wedding. A woman she'd befriended in
the orchard, not a Mennonite, was getting married. It
was her second marriage.

My father refused to go. He said people were
allowed only one wedding. "You make that one work,
or you spend the rest of your days thinking about
your mistake," he said to us.

"What about if your husband beats you," I said to
my dad, "or robs banks or grows a second head?" He
wasn't sure if I was talking back or trying to make
him laugh, so he didn't say anything else. I was talking back, no question. I was learning that there were
more ways than the one way my father believed in.

He didn't want my mom to go to the wedding.
Maybe he felt left out because he didn't know her
friend. They had met picking cherries and spent the
summer talking in trees, where you could say a lot of
things you might not say in a living room.

We took my dad's car. He wasn't happy about us

going to the wedding, but he said he couldn't tell my mom what to do. "Her first husband did beat her," my mom told me on the way to the wedding in Grimsby. "If supper wasn't ready or his shirts weren't ironed. For some reason his mother never loved him, wouldn't hug him as a boy. He never learned to love. That's no excuse, though, for treating his wife like that."

"Is she sure that her new husband is better?" I asked.

"She says he worships the ground she walks on," my mom replied. "And kisses her so much she has to say stop."

I giggled. "Aren't they your age? Too old!"

My mother shot a sideways glance at me from the driver's seat. Her hands gripped the steering wheel tightly. "You're never too old for affection, my girl. See how Tante Tina cuddles you."

"But that's different," I protested.

"Maybe so," said my mom. "Maybe not."

We drove along the Welland ship canal and over the escarpment and above the high, flat plane of farmland to Grimsby. The Old Number 8 highway wound through lush green landscapes, little patches of dense forest, old towns tucked between the woods and the farms. Neat orchards with tidy rows melted into towering oaks sheltering big brick houses. All along the way, there were fruit stands displaying wooden baskets overflowing with shiny red cherries, pink plums, orange apricots, and early peaches.

We stopped at one stand advertising fruit nectar

and sipped a cool glass of homemade cherry juice. It was a gentle day, not too humid. A little breeze brought scents of grass and roses to us.

We arrived at noon. My mother's friend, Lily, greeted us with kisses. She wore a long yellow dress and daisies in her hair. She wasn't fat, but big in front. Her fiancé was a bearded man, Hungarian he told us. He was jovial, florid, and happy. It was true about the kisses. He grabbed my mom's cheeks and kissed each one with a resounding smack, then kissed Lily twice before reaching for me.

I ducked and held out my hand instead. He smiled and bowed and kissed it, welcomed us gallantly, then gathered Lily into his arms again and said it was the happiest day of his life. I wasn't used to men making such a fuss about being happy, or about loving a woman.

They led us into the backyard where people were setting up chairs. There were flowers everywhere. Gladiolas and roses, four o'clocks and petunias, and dozens of other flowers I couldn't identify filled the garden with colour and the air with perfume. People milled around and three old men stood in the shade of a maple tree sipping mugs of beer. Beside them, on a table, lay their instruments and, as soon as they drained their glasses, they swiped at their faces with the backs of their hands and began making music on accordion, violin, and guitar.

I took a seat beside a girl my age in a geranium red dress. She held a bouquet of irises in her hand. It was her name too, Iris. I was jealous of her pretty name.

"If my mom has a girl," she told us, "we're going to call her Rose."

So this was Lily's daughter! Though her mom was as old as mine, she was having a new baby! These people didn't seem to be following the rules at all, and still they seemed perfectly happy. I tried to picture my mother pregnant and happy, pink-cheeked, and kissable. I couldn't.

Iris left me to join her mother. Mom came and sat beside me. The three old musicians were surprisingly limber. They played their instruments with ease and turned the wedding into a celebration.

A woman minister in a white robe listened to the couple's vows and pronounced them husband and wife. The audience cheered and whistled as Lily's new husband, one hand on Lily's stomach and the other in her hair, kissed his bride. Then he made a fist and shook it at the three old men, who broke into a reel of joy that brought the guests to their feet and into a circle.

It happened so naturally that my mother and I were swept up in it and though we didn't know the steps, we were dancing too! It was easy, arms around your neighour, feet moving to the left, once in front, then behind, a swivel of the hips, and do it all again. People shouted and whooped, the circle spun slowly, the music and the scent of flowers made me dizzy. I loved it.

Then the circle broke into couples and everybody

knew the dance, even the kids, except me and my mom. We watched while the lawn flashed with whirling pairs and stamping feet and clapping hands. The three musicians smiled at us and bowed over their instruments. Then Iris came by and grabbed my hand and showed me that this dance was easy too. Each verse was a little different, but the chorus was always the same and the music made moving irresistible.

I watched my mother. Every time a new dance started another man would show her the steps. She was clumsy compared to the people who had been dancing all their lives, but she was flushed and happy, and when she caught my eyes she smiled.

We danced until the food was brought out and set onto long tables in the shade. Then we ate and drank. Voices rose. People laughed and shouted and drank homemade wine from tumblers in the middle of the day. The three old men played all afternoon and there was always someone dancing.

On the way home, we were quiet for a while, a companionable silence between us like jam in a sandwich. Then I started smiling wide at the memory of my mom dancing with an old man, and I laughed. She looked at me sideways, then lifted her hands from the steering wheel briefly to clap them once above her head.

"In church they always tell us that dancing is bad," I said to my mom. "In Young People's the leader said dancing could lead to sex." I thought of the children beside their parents in the circle dance, of the old man who shuffled my mother through the steps, and of the couples who waltzed together on the lawn between the flowers and the guests.

"Well," my mother said, her hands holding the steering wheel tightly. "I guess they just don't know how to dance."

"Do you wish Dad would dance with you sometimes?" I asked her.

At first she smiled, then her smile disappeared slowly.

"I don't think he would be a very good dancer," she said. "I'm not."

"You were great, Mom," I said. But her awkward movements were stiff compared to the fluid grace of the people who'd been doing it all their lives.

"What was your wedding dress like?" I asked my mom.

"It had twenty-five buttons down the back, and I hated it," my mom said. "I couldn't do it myself. My mother had to button it up."

"Who unbuttoned it?" I asked, giggling, and shut my ears like I didn't really want to hear the answer.

She shook her head at me. "My sister, Lena. I changed into my going-away suit after the wedding and then we went on our honeymoon."

"You and your sister?" I laughed again.

She ignored me. "My going-away outfit was olive green. And I had spike-heeled, pointy-toed shoes exactly the same colour. And a little hat."

I was shocked. I didn't know my mom had been so stylish.

"I had a nice figure in those days," she added. "Your dad liked my legs in the high heels. We went to Burlington for our honeymoon."

Burlington was next to the steel mills of Hamilton, famous for its sulphur smoke and pollution in the lake.

"In those days, rich people kept holiday homes beside the Burlington Bay," she said. "We stayed at a bed and breakfast in a big house with a fancy veranda, big trees in the yard. They brought us orange juice and melons in the morning and we had breakfast in bed. That was the first and last time. I didn't really like it, all those crumbs on the sheets."

"But it's so romantic," I said.

"Well, here comes my favourite part of the honeymoon," she said. "There was a Mennonite choir gathering in Hamilton that weekend. People came from all around Canada to sing together. That's why we went to Burlington."

"So you spent your honeymoon weekend with about a hundred other Mennonites," I said, disappointed.

"Actually, about a thousand. In those days there were lots more Mennonites. And boy, did they love to sing!"

"So you spent your whole honeymoon singing hymns." I couldn't believe it.

"Yes," she answered. "Your dad loved it. He was so

proud. Proud of his new wife. Proud of his fine tenor voice. Proud to be on his honeymoon." She smiled, and though the memory was a happy one, her voice shook like she was sad.

When we got home, my dad was in the kitchen, reading the Saturday newspaper and drinking coffee. My mother kissed the top of his head where it was balding and sat down at the table with him. She placed her folded hands in front of her.

"It was fun, Dad!" I spoke without thinking. "I bet you didn't know that Mom's a great dancer!" He shook his head.

"I guess there's a lot about your mom I don't know anymore," he said.

She looked at her hands. It looked like she was going to pray, but she didn't say anything at all. My dad got up and poured her a cup of coffee, added some cream, and set it down roughly in front of her. Some coffee splashed out of the cup and onto the table. She smiled at him as he returned to his seat, put her hand on his briefly.

Then she got up. "Let's show him how it went," my mom said to me. I took her outstretched hand and we did the dance where the feet went forward and back and the arms waved side to side. It was an easy one, a line dance, but I couldn't imagine my father joining us, lifting his hands above his head and letting them fall. My mom was smiling again, though not as wide as at the wedding.

"Your friend Lily married the right guy," I said.

"He knows how to make her smile. If I ever get married, that's what my man will have to be good at."

Then I clowned for my father, kicking my feet up high and waving my hands like Chris saying bye-bye, and he did finally crack a smile. Then he got serious again and watched my mother, who sipped her coffee and mopped up the spill with her handkerchief.

VERENEKE

The rest of Sunday was quiet and boring. Compared to Tante Tina's place, not much happened at home. I always looked forward to Monday mornings.

At Tante Tina's, my days were so full that I was tired at night. When I closed my eyes at the end of those long, hot, humid days, images of green leaves, of long garden rows, of ripe red berries imprinted on my eyelids. I fell asleep as soon as I wiggled my feet out the bottom of my blankets. I woke knowing that every day was a whole new world.

My hair had always been short, but early that summer, when I first passed a comb through Tante Tina's waist-length grey hair, rippled from the twists and folds of her bun, I vowed to grow mine. Now it hung in my eyes, long enough to tuck behind my ears, not quite long enough to tie back. I endured it, imagined the feel of it on my shoulder blades and back, like water falling.

Each day with Tante Tina was fun. We laughed

before breakfast, ate with abandon. There were very few rules. "I'm too old to do as I should," Tante Tina said to me between smiles. "And you might as well get a head start on that."

Some days we ate only fruit and vegetables from the garden. As the summer progressed, we feasted on sweet apricots cool with morning dew for breakfast, carrots and cucumbers and peas for lunch, sweet cherries anytime, sliced peaches with ice cream in the cool of sundown. We shared all our meals and I felt healthy and strong.

I forgot to worry. Before, there was always something to worry about – a Bible verse that spoke to me, a rule I'd broken, something I'd done wrong, whether or not I was saved, whether I would wake up the next morning, whether Jesus would return in a moment that I wasn't ready.

Now I even forgot to bite my fingernails. They grew long, were always black with dirt from the garden. I hardly recognized myself in the mirror. I felt wild, and very free.

It had been a particularly hot early August day, too hot to work outside, so Tante Tina and I sat in the cool of her breezeway. The big oak tree planted outside her front door shaded the house. We sipped ginger ale over ice cubes, enjoying a well-deserved rest. We had been busy.

The shelves of her pantry were stocked with jars of

preserves. We'd canned the first peaches of August, succulent globes of golden fruit that slipped out of their prickly jackets after a quick blanching. Jars of pickled cucumbers lined the shelves, the tiny, warty creatures floating in pickling brine decorated with dill. Strawberry, apricot, plum, and rhubarb jams shone like rubies, garnets, and amethysts. The freezer was filling with carrots, beans, and peas that we cooked, cut, and froze. The corn in the garden was high and green, with golden plumes beginning to blacken.

Today Tante Tina promised we would make one of her specialties – sweet *vereneke,* tiny dough pockets stuffed with sour cherries. She made a sweet cream gravy to go with it. It was my absolute favourite food in the world. Now, however, we were sitting, motion-less, in the shade of her front porch.

"When I'm here, I'm not afraid of anything," I said to my Tante Tina.

"What's there to be afraid of, *Miale?*" she asked me, wiping the drop of sweat that trickled down her lined throat toward her breasts.

I couldn't answer right away. None of it made sense after my summer of living with her. "Mostly I'm afraid that I won't do the right thing," I admitted finally. "And that I'll go to hell."

"Nah, what kind of a God would send a good girl like you to hell?" Tante Tina looked at me over the rim of her glass. "And with such a good name as Tina, too. My girl, you don't have to worry about that!"

I laughed with her. "Let's go teach you to make those *vereneke,*" Tante Tina told me. "But you have to promise to keep the recipe secret until you have a daughter. This is a very special treat, and people will come from far and wide to beg you for the recipe. But it is yours, and yours alone."

"I don't think I'll ever have a daughter," I told my aunt, but I agreed to keep the secret. Anything for a taste of my favourite food.

We mixed flour, baking powder, salt, eggs, and fresh cream into a dough. It took work to get it just the right amount of sticky. After leaving it alone for an hour, we rolled it out, cut it into squares, dropped the sour cherry filling in the middle, folded over the dough, and pinched the edges tight. Then we boiled the dumplings in the big pot we used for steaming shut the pickles. While we waited for the *vereneke* to cook, we sat outside in the wooden swing.

I took a deep breath.

"Tante Tina," I said as we rocked back and forth in the creaky swing, "why didn't you let your daughters visit my Opa?"

"Nah, *Miale,* how do you know this story?"

I didn't want to get my mother in trouble, so I shrugged my shoulders and waited without speaking.

"You want to know too much," she said to me. By the way her bun was vibrating, I could tell she was angry. But she calmed down when I remained silent. *"Nah ja.* I made it my duty to always answer my girls. If they had a question about anything," and here she

146

glared at me, "I would answer as good as I could."

"Some people say you fell in love with a German soldier. Other people say you were raped." I'd never said that word before and it made my throat feel tight and sore. "But nobody could tell me why you hate your brother."

Tina breathed hard out her nose. "It was so long ago," she said, "that it really doesn't matter. I'm a grandmother now. Not every question has an answer and mystery is the pepper of life."

She got up abruptly, and went into the house to check on the *vereneke*. I didn't move, didn't even rock the swing. I wished she wouldn't be mad at me, but I'd had to ask.

Tante Tina returned, holding a plate with four steaming dumplings, smothered in a sweet creamy gravy. She sat down beside me and we ate the *vereneke* together.

"My mother says these are too hard to make," I told Tante Tina. "But you make it seem easy."

Tante Tina sighed. "If I don't tell you," she said to me, "then you will make up a thousand and one stories. I'm going to tell you this because you asked, not because I think this is a story to tell a girl who's not even sixteen."

She stopped then, remembered something, and added, "Although at sixteen I was already grown up."

She began. *"Ach,* it was a terrible time to be alive. The terrible famines of the 1930s were followed by the war. We tried to keep out of the way of the soldiers, to farm and stay quiet, but we had three strikes against us. We owned land, we were farmers, and we were religious. All against Stalin's policies. We lived in fear, every day. We couldn't trust the Russians. Stalin was the devil himself. Many Mennonites were pulled from their beds at night and sent to work camps in Siberia.

"Our parents," she added significantly. "We never saw them again. Your Opa and I, we just wanted to leave those troubles behind. Germany was where we thought we would be safe. And free. So your Opa and Oma and I, and your dad and his brother and sister joined the German soldiers who were returning to their country after their defeat at Moscow.

"It was not a pretty sight, our trek across Russia and into Poland. We had nothing, no food, no money. Just an old cart and an old horse, some woollen blankets, and what we could beg and borrow and steal. We raided gardens along the way, for potatoes and beets and turnips, made soup at night over tiny fires. It was so cold and there was so little to eat that the two little ones – your dad's brother and sister – caught diphtheria and died. *Shrecklich*. There are no good memories from that time.

"The army travelled in front of us. For some reason, the soldiers hated my brother, your Opa. Maybe they knew his true nature. That he would do anything to survive. That he was a coward. Which he proved to be. One day when we were cold and hungry and tired, we came to a deserted farmyard. At least we thought

148

it was deserted, until the soldiers broke the house door down and found the Polish family hiding inside in the dark, cold house. The youngest child was cowering at the bottom of the flour barrel. The soldiers ordered my brother to shoot the family.

"I stamped my feet and shouted, 'No!' And that's when one soldier hit me with his gun, and worse. When I woke up, I was in the barn, lying in straw mixed with my blood. I didn't know it, but I was pregnant. The soldiers were inside the house, burning chairs and table legs in the oven, eating roasted potatoes and the last two skinny chickens they'd found in the yard. The Polish family was gone, gone to heaven, I guess, and I have never forgiven my brother for not refusing to murder."

"He killed those people?" My mouth was dry and I had goosebumps on every part of my skin.

"Nah," my aunt grimaced. "I will never know, really, but this is how I answer your question. I hope you're not too sorry you asked. Curiosity killed the cat, they say."

I couldn't answer. It was too terrible. No wonder my Opa was haunted. No wonder he was so mean and cruel, to kittens and to me.

"Nah, Miale, come sit by me." I scooted across, and slid into the swing beside her. She moved over and the boards were warm from her body. I sat as close as I could. Despite the afternoon heat, I was suddenly cold. We sat quietly without talking for a long time. My father was due to pick me up to take

me home for the weekend. I was in no hurry.

The afternoon shadows lengthened. In the distance, thunder rumbled, like the growling of a hungry stomach. Lightning sizzled on the hazy horizon. In the dim summer dusk, my fear was as big as the universe.

But as I sat there, my sweaty skin pressed against my great-aunt's warmth, I felt that I was expanding. With each breath I got bigger, until I was so big that I could hold the terror and the hate and the fear. And at the same time I remembered that we were making *vereneke* and that they were one of my favourite foods and that I could eat some more later with sweet cream gravy. The swing creaked as my aunt rocked us. A breeze sprang up. I was amazed that I could contain this story without bursting. I had to cry, though, for the little boy hiding at the bottom of the barrel.

Tante Tina absorbed my tears with her sleeve and stroked my hair, tucked my bangs behind my ears and said, "Your hair will soon be as long as mine."

I laughed through my sobs. "Not for years and years," I said. "Your hair is down to your bum."

"Well, your bum isn't as far from your hair as mine is," she chuckled. I pressed myself into her warm, solid flesh, tightening my arms around her.

She held me for another moment, then raised my face and touched her nose to mine. "Let's get you fixed up. If your dad sees you like this, he'll never let you come back."

She pulled a comb from her hair and neatened my

hair, and scrubbed my face with her apron, moistening a corner of it in her mouth and gently washing the skin around my eyes.

Then she took my hand and pulled me up and into the house.

"You give these *vereneke* to your mama, then she won't have to make supper tomorrow. She must miss her girl."

Suddenly I felt terribly guilty. I hadn't thought about my mother in a week, not since the wedding last weekend. I didn't miss her at all. I didn't worry about the extra work the baby was making for her. I was so happy with Tante Tina that I'd even fantasized she was my mother. That made me feel guilty too.

"Do I have to keep the recipe a secret even from my mother?"

Tina nodded at me, and then winked. "Well, if she asks you nicely, you can tell her."

We moved to the breezeway and waited for my dad. The distant lightning came closer, bringing rain. The wind blew in through the screen, thick and wet, smelling of summer earth and wet grass. I didn't want this moment to go. Just then my father drove up, his headlights cutting a bright swath through the damp, grey air.

He looked tired. "I had to work overtime," he said. "They're training us to use the new machines. But we still had to do it the old way too. That's why I'm late."

"We know what the General's like," I said to him,

trying to tease a smile out of him, but he was all worn out.

"Well," Tante Tina said, "you're just in time. After working hard all day, we made a big pot of *vereneke*. Tina's going to be a better cook than me soon."

She winked at me and handed me the package of food. My father and I walked out the door into the warm rain. I felt drops on my face, stopped, couldn't move for a moment. The rain falling on my face felt like flower petals. My dad got into the car and turned the engine on and honked the horn at me, startling me so that I started crying again.

My father sighed and shrugged his shoulders. "What's the matter, Tina?" he called from the car.

"She's growing up," answered my aunt from the breezeway door. "Be nice to her. She's almost a woman."

That made my father uncomfortable, and he was quiet during the ride home.

GROWING UP

My mother was sitting at the kitchen table when we arrived. It was warm in the house, and close. I gave her a hug and went around opening windows. She was strangely quiet, not even excited about the special *vereneke*. I put them in the fridge and peeked into Mary Anne's room. The light was out and Chris was crying. Mary Anne put her finger to her lips when she saw me in the light of the doorway. She was too busy with Chris to talk with me.

My parents' clean, new house had the feeling of a Sears' catalogue. Tante Tina's house was old and much more comfortable to live in. I went upstairs to my room, but it was too hot to sleep. I lay on my bed and listened to the foghorn wail over Lake Ontario. I didn't feel at home in my home anymore; maybe this was what it was like to grow up.

I heard my parents getting ready for bed. And then my mother knocked on my door.

"Come in," I said. She sat down on the edge of my bed in the dark. "The foghorn is so sad tonight," I said. "It's worse than the organ in church."

My mother looked at her hands, cleaned one of her nails, then said, suddenly, "Your dad wants his father to come and live with us."

Everything was changing.

"Opa! Come here?" I was shocked. "But you don't like Opa," I blurted out, not knowing how to say the other things about him.

My mother said, "Shhh. It's Dad's dad, you know, you have to be nice. He's getting too sick to live at home alone, so he'll come and live here in the spare room."

I could tell that Opa coming to live here wasn't her idea, but she was going along with my dad. That's what you had to do when you were married.

"But all his stupid pigeons won't fit in there," I said. "And he'll stink up the whole place with his shitty boots. And I won't be able to bring my friends home!"

My mother said, "Shhh. He's Dad's father." This time she emphasized the word father, to remind me that family loyalty was important.

"Why do *you* have to take care of him? Why can't he go to the hospital or an old folks' home, or to jail? I don't want him here!" I was furious, felt my cheeks blossom with heat. I was going to cry in a minute, and my mother looked at me strangely, as though she didn't recognize me.

"Tina," my mother said, "you never liked him, even when you were a little girl. Maybe you just have to change your mind about him."

"Never," I said, and I could feel my face get hot. "He shouldn't be near Chris. I saw him kill some kittens, just like it was nothing. He could do the same to Chris, maybe to me and to you. We won't be safe here."

"Shh!" My mother looked horrified.

"Tante Tina told me stories about him. He killed people," I said to her.

"People did terrible things in those days," my mother said woodenly. "Just to stay alive."

"Maybe he could go live with Tante Tina," I said. "She's his sister. She could take care of him." I knew, though, that Tante Tina would never do it, and I knew why.

"She doesn't even let him come onto her yard," my mother said. "Do you think he could stay in her house?"

"Well, then, maybe I'll go live with Tante Tina." I knew I was going to be sorry for what I was about to say. "I wish she was my mother, anyway." As soon as the words were out of my mouth, I saw that they were painful. I saw my mother flinch. Tears gathered in her eyes. I wanted to say I was sorry, but I was too mad. Why wouldn't she stand up to my dad? Why didn't she know that I hated Opa? And why I hated him.

"Nobody likes the old man," I said, calmer. "Why do we have to be the ones to take care of him? It's not fair. I bet you'll have to do it all. Dad's not going to give him medicine or help him go to the bathroom. You have to make him go somewhere else. He can't live here."

I was starting to feel hysterical. I felt as though I wouldn't be able to stop myself from saying what I had to say. I had stopped it for too long. Everybody around me had secrets about the old man and nobody would tell the truth about him. At the same time, they told me I shouldn't lie and that if I did, Jesus would know and I would go to hell. Straight to hell – do not pass go, do not collect $200. There was nothing I wanted more than to have been born anything or anybody but a Mennonite. None of it made any sense at all. I despised the hypocrisy.

"You have to make allowances for the old man," my mother spoke quietly. It didn't sound as though she believed what she was saying, but she said it anyway. "He's old and sick, and he's your Dad's dad."

There didn't seem to be a way out of this situation. My mother had memorized her reasons like I'd memorized John 3:16 in Sunday School. I knew she wasn't even hearing her own words.

"I'm going to have to tell Dad all the bad things he did. I'll tell Mary Anne too and everyone at school. I'll go in front of the church like Mary Anne had to when they made her beg them for forgiveness." I wanted to confide in my mother, but I couldn't tell my mother about the bad things he had done to me.

"Tina!" My mother was angry now.

"What?"

"You scare me, Tina. I don't know how to control you."

"I don't want you to control me. Just love me. Like

Tante Tina does. She's not afraid of me. She makes me laugh."

"I don't know how to make you laugh anymore," my mom said. "You're not my little girl anymore."

"I am," I said. "I am yours, but I'm not a little girl anymore." I felt grown up when I said those words.

She looked at me, steady and serious and said, "I know. You are growing up. But you are mine! I'm glad you're not Tante Tina's girl."

"Me too," I said. She kissed me on top of my head, tucked my hair behind my ears. "Your hair has grown," she said as she left. "We'll have to get you a haircut."

"I'm growing it, Mom. By Christmas it's gonna be down to my bum. You'll see."

She looked at me again, and said, "I hope that by Christmas, my girl, some things will have changed. Good night."

She didn't say what would change, but I trusted that she would do the right thing for me. After all, I was her girl.

I had a dream that night, a bad dream, the same bad dream I'd been having since I was a kid.

I was on a beach, having fun, and then an old man with white hair came up to me and ordered me to pick up all the sand on the beach. He ordered me to put it into a bucket. When I said no, he twisted my ear until I said okay. But I couldn't do it. It was too big a job. But he said I had to do it. And he waited until I started. I dropped the grains of sand into the bucket, one by one. I looked up and the expanse of beach stretched to infinity. It was too great a task, but the old man threatened me. I woke up and my fists were clenched and my heart was beating hard.

When I was younger, I use to go to my parents' bedroom when I woke up from this dream, but today I just lay in my bed, sweating, listening to my heart pound. It was hot and humid. I could hear the foghorn wailing over the lake. I thought of the lakers out on the water, travelling across Lake Ontario on their way to the St. Lawrence River, and then to the ocean. The thought of all that open water helped me breathe better, and after a while I fell asleep.

THE ANGEL

The next day was still hot, too hot. Yesterday's little thunderstorm hadn't broken the humidity. Chris's fussing woke me up early in the morning, when the sun was just rising, a hot, red ball above the horizon. I smelled coffee, then I heard my dad leave for work and I fell asleep again.

When I finally got up, the sun was much higher in the sky. Mary Anne dressed Chris in a white T-shirt and pink terry cloth shorts. The rest of us wore shorts too and Mary Anne wore a halter top. My mom and Mary Anne said they were too hot to eat, but I was hungry. I made a fruit salad with fresh apricots, peaches, and plums. Everybody ate some anyway.

"Today's the day," said my mom. "We'll go to Aunt Lena's and deal with the garden." Peas, beans, corn, zucchini, cucumbers, carrots, and tomatoes had ripened in the summer's heat and humidity. My mom and her sister always worked together to can and freeze their garden vegetables. All of us except my dad were going. I wasn't really looking forward to seeing

Lorraine, but so much had happened since I'd last seen her that I thought everything might be all right. We all piled into the car and drove to my aunt Lena's place, on the outskirts of Homer, along the same creek that Anna's family lived on, only farther away from the lake, nearer the Niagara Escarpment.

Nobody came outside to greet us, but when we got to the front door, Lorraine was there, opening it for us. We said hi, warily. She peered at Chris, who waved her arms and arched her back and gave Lorraine a big smile. Lorraine smiled back, and looked up, surprised. Then our mothers shooed us into the garden, while they and Mary Anne disappeared into the kitchen to wash and sterilize bottles and prepare for canning. They would can peaches in the morning and planned to preserve the vegetables in the afternoon.

Lorraine and I spent the morning picking, each of us starting in opposite corners of the garden and working our way to the middle. We worked together in the mounting heat, bending over the green rows. At first there was an uncomfortable silence between us and we didn't talk much, but after a while we both had things to complain about.

"Why do people plant their gardens so far away from the shade?" I asked. "I wish someone planted a big willow tree right in the middle, to cool me off."

"I'm never going to have a garden when I'm grown up," Lorraine vowed.

By early afternoon, we had filled many baskets full

of fresh vegetables. "You've worked so hard," said my mom, proudly. "The boat will be your reward." Lorraine's brothers had built a wooden rowboat when they were kids. I loved to paddle it down the creek.

"It'll be so nice and cool on the creek," said my aunt Lena.

Mary Anne smiled encouragingly while feeding Chris.

Lorraine rolled her eyes. She didn't seem particularly interested in going out in the boat. She probably thought she was too old and sophisticated to play in a boat. But the option of spending the afternoon boiling and steaming and canning in the hot kitchen and helping like Mary Anne wasn't very appealing either.

To me, being in the boat on the creek was the best treat I could imagine. My mom had the right idea. "Great!" I said, tickling Chris's toes and making her laugh. After a late lunch of buns with cheese and fresh tomatoes, we were free to go.

Lorraine and I climbed into the boat and nosed it upstream, paddling against the creek as it flowed from the escarpment to the lake. We turned into a cool side channel that I'd never before explored. Giant oaks, tall willows, and elegant poplars shaded the creamy brown water. There was a certain smell on the creek – last year's leaves were musky, and this year's tangled, brambly growth had a fresh, green scent. Blackberry bushes with not quite ripe berries climbed the hillsides above the creek. Manitoba

maple and sumac trees and wild grapes and tall thistles with bristling purple flowers grew thickly along
the creek's banks. A few old apple trees gone wild
dropped their knobby green fruits into the water. A
broken willow trunk made a perfect bench at creek's
edge.

The day's humidity had built and the afternoon
was heavy and sleepy. We'd devoured fresh peaches in
the boat, drooling juice overboard. Big yellow carp
passed by and we laughed at their fat, sluggish swimming.

At this moment, it felt all right to be with
Lorraine. In the boat, all the other stuff that had happened at school dissolved, or at least faded into the
distance. We were just cousins, and that meant we
had to live with each other.

"Chris is cute," Lorraine said.

I looked up from watching the brown water break
against the bow of the boat.

"Yeah, we think so too."

"I like the way she tries to hold her head up. She
smiled at me."

"When she smiles at me, it feels like the best present ever."

"What's it like having her in the house?"

"Just like having another sister. But Mary Anne
mostly takes care of her. I haven't been home much
this summer anyway."

It was easy to talk. School and church didn't exist
on the creek. We floated for a while, not talking.

On the water it was cool and refreshing. Beneath the willows we didn't notice the sky go grey. Thunder erupted in the distance above the lake. Lorraine and I paddled further upstream, suddenly realizing it was getting dark. Lightning touched our eyes like fireflies. We could smell a fruit dump. As we neared the rot, we heard the harmony of flies.

The ride ended abruptly when the boat's snub nose bumped against a log across the creek. We nearly tipped over. We laughed at first, but sobered up quickly when the thunder snapped at us like an angry preacher. Lightning fingered the peach trees that stood in their regimented rows.

We brought the boat to the bank. In the growing dark we pulled the boat's snout out of the creek, tied its rope to the nearest tree and walked, barefoot, into the orchard. The foghorn over Lake Ontario moaned low and slow, sadder even than the song of our church organ during an altar call. Fear grabbed me then, for some reason. I froze. In the dim light I thought I heard voices on the air.

"I'm scared," Lorraine said, in my ear. She wasn't afraid to admit it. "Let's get out of here!" She ran toward the boat and I started to follow her. But as I watched, ahead in the shadows, I saw her fall to the ground as an angel appeared, a long-limbed, white-winged creature that hovered above the peach trees, braiding its tail into the branches.

"Lorraine!" I called. She didn't answer.

Then it looked like the lake burst into flames

behind me. I saw the flash of trumpets like teeth in Satan's smile. I called Lorraine again. My voice ricocheted between us. I could only think of the warmth of a calf's mouth, the heat and strength of its tongue when it sucked on my hands. I longed for the careless indifference of Mietze's tail.

Had I seen an angel? Was it the end of the world?

I called Lorraine again and ran toward her, squatted on the ground beside her. "I fell," she said, brushing orchard dirt from her leg. Her knee was scraped and bleeding. "And look what I found. It's disgusting," she said, pointing to a tiny creature on the ground, a small, bald baby rabbit decorated with a bloody gash. Its chest hollowed and heaved with hurting breath and in its eyes I saw my terror.

"The owl dropped it," Lorraine cried.

The owl. No angel. Was there nothing to fear after all? The foghorn wailed its warning to ships in the middle of the lonely lake, and I put my finger on the rabbit's forehead. The animal panicked at my touch and writhed. Its blood clotted with the orchard dirt and its back legs convulsed. Thunder rumbled, close at hand.

Lorraine got up to leave, limping as she walked toward the boat. "Come on," she said. "That's gross. And my knee is sore. Let's go."

"In a minute," I answered. I couldn't leave the rabbit like this. I had to do something good for the little creature. "I'm going to put it out of its misery."

If I didn't, how long would the poor little thing

suffer? I picked up the tiny creature and squeezed the life out of it as lightning lit up the sky and made grotesque statues of the peach trees. Then I rolled the rabbit on the ground and its blood soaked up the earth.

The owl hooted overhead and I began to cry. Didn't my Opa do the same thing? Didn't he kill defenceless little creatures? Did that mean I was the same as him? I choked on my tears, gasped, pressed my forehead to the ground and breathed the thick smell of orchard earth. It helped.

As I picked up the body and carried it to a crotch of a cherry tree and covered it with leaves, I reminded myself that I was only helping the creature. My thought was punctuated with an exclamation of lightning, and a crack of thunder. I walked back to the boat, silently, my mind full of thoughts. Lorraine had pushed the boat into the water and was waiting for me.

"How could you do that?" she asked as we climbed aboard.

"I couldn't just leave it."

She nodded, like she agreed. "I couldn't do it. Let's get out of here."

Lightning flashed and thunder growled, but the storm seemed to be moving away as we pushed off against the bank and dug our paddles into the water to propel us into the current. I felt the first cool raindrops land on my hot cheeks. The storm would clear the air and bring coolness and relief after the hot days of late August. Lorraine and I paddled easily without talking. Sometimes we drifted with the current. Rain dropped on us. Soon my mind was wiped clean by the cool drops of water. It was not the end of the world, after all. And I had done a good thing for the rabbit. I was not bad like my Opa. In the nearly dark, the rain rolled down my face, cleansing me and relieving me of my fears.

It was late and dark when we got back to Lorraine's house. Our mothers sat at the kitchen table cutting long golden strips of corn kernels off their cobs. Mary Anne spooned corn into plastic bags for freezing. The house was hot with humidity and the boiling, but the clean smell of rain through the wide open windows was in there too. Chris slept in her blanket on the sofa. I thought of Christmas dinner, a feast with turkey, *bubbat* stuffing, gravy, and a steaming spoonful of this summer gold speckled with black pepper.

Lorraine and I were hungry after our adventure on the creek. We grabbed hot cobs of corn from the pot, pressed them into the butter, and sank our teeth into the sweet, juicy flesh. We chewed with open mouths.

"We were worried about you girls out in that storm," said my aunt Lena.

"You could have been struck by lightning," said my mom.

"But we weren't," said Lorraine.

"I thought I saw an angel," I admitted, wiping my

buttery fingers on a kitchen towel. "Then I thought the lake was on fire and it was the end of the world."

"She's got an imagination, that one," said my aunt Lena, jerking her chin toward me.

My mother shook her head a bit sadly, as though she was sorry for me.

"The thunder woke Chris up," said Mary Anne. "But she didn't even cry. She just lay there listening."

"It was a good storm," I said. "Everything's more peaceful now."

"And cooler," said Lorraine, fanning the air with her corncob.

"Cooler," repeated my mom. Everyone agreed, nodding at each other over the steaming pots and open plastic bags of corn.

I thought we would tell our mothers about the owl and the rabbit, but Lorraine didn't talk about it. I kept it a secret too. After all, I was growing up, and didn't have to tell my mother everything.

The next day was Sunday and my father said I should go to church with him. He said the church service was a special one. "All about the end times and Armageddon," he told me. "There's a special preacher."

I wasn't eager to hear more about the end times, when Jesus would gather all the Christians into heaven and then withdraw from the earth and loose the devil upon the world for a thousand years, a thousand years without God's love. This particular part of the

Bible always made me feel like I wasn't good enough, no matter how I tried. But I went because my father asked me to go with him.

They sure got their money's worth with this preacher. He was fiery and passionate. His voice broke sometimes and he pounded the pulpit for emphasis. He described hell and warned that it was easy to end up there. I didn't want to listen, but every time I closed my eyes I saw myself descending stone stairs into an eternal eruption of flames. Forever was a long time. I considered my faults.

I talked back to my mom and hated my Opa. I was vain, and spent hours looking at myself in the mirror, often without clothes. I liked to touch myself, all over. I knew, at the very bottom of it all, I was bad. And, worst of all, I knew in my heart, where Jesus was supposed to be, that I wasn't saved. I had tried, over and over, to become born again, like they said, but it never worked. Even as a young child, I doubted.

Instead of listening to the preacher, I remembered a time when I was ten years old. I had come home from school to find no one home. Clearly, I thought, Jesus had returned and I was the only one left on earth. There was going to be weeping and wailing and gnashing of teeth, I knew that for sure. At first I felt like crying, but then I called Anna. She was the best person I knew, and her younger brothers were too young to go to hell – there was a certain cut-off age where you were automatically saved. If they were all at home, then I was safe.

Anna answered the phone. I could hear her brothers fighting in the background. I faked some questions about math homework, and felt a great relief, although my heart didn't stop racing for a long time.

Another day I was awakened at sunrise by trumpets – the last trump, the announcement of Christ's return to earth. Though it had been preached to me since I was a child, I never thought that it would really happen! I lay under my covers in my flannel nightgown, shivering and waiting. "Low in the Grave He Lay," the trumpets moaned. I had to pee but I couldn't move. I had gone to bed without underwear, and I wished now that I'd worn some. You just never knew when Jesus would return.

They said that the dead Christians would rise up to meet him first, and after that Christians on earth would join the heavenly throng. I lay there, hoping desperately that I might begin floating. But I was bedbound, without even the tiniest liftoff.

The song ended, and the trumpets blasted the refrains of "On a hill far away stood an old rugged cross, the emblem of suffering and shame." I remembered how Jesus had suffered before he died. I felt bad for him. I didn't want to suffer. I wasn't ready to die.

The urge to pee became so strong that I had to get up and do something about it. My feet touched the cool linoleum of my bedroom floor. I crept to the window, expecting to see multitudes. Would the dead in Christ have replaced their flesh, or would it be a gathering of ghouls?

The yard below me was empty of everything but grass. My eyes travelled beyond, to the street where two lone figures stood playing trumpet. A watery sun poked long, pale fingers into the budding branches of a birch tree which cast grotesque morning shadows through my many-paned window. I saw not angels after all, but two men playing trumpets, Harry Dyck and his second cousin, Henry Froese. I remembered then that it was Easter Sunday. This must be their idea of an Easter treat.

All that morning at church, people from our street thanked the two trumpeters. I refused to look at them, consoled myself at lunchtime with generous portions of *paska*, a sweet Easter bread baked in a coffee tin, spread thickly with butter, my favourite thing about Easter.

My mind came back to the present moment when the preacher's voice rose for the altar call. He begged us to repent. "Stand and follow the spirit, brothers and sisters. Show the Lord that you are His." The church organist played "Just as I Am," more sorrowfully than I'd ever heard it played before.

My heart was beating like a jackhammer. "Should I go?" I asked my father.

"If the Holy Spirit is leading you," he answered.

At that, I almost leaped to my feet and ran to the

front, so strong was my fear, but I forced myself to stay sitting. I thought about how I felt. This feeling inside me now was no more the Holy Spirit than yesterday's owl had been an angel. It was more like holy terror.

The American minister said Hallelujah, Amen, and Praise Jesus several times as two of the toughest guys in Young People's walked sheepishly down the aisle. Brother Wilf, a missionary on furlough from Zaire, met them at the front of the church, and ushered them out to the Young People's room where they would kneel and pray and ask Jesus into their hearts.

I pressed my palm against my chest. My heart was still beating hard, but it was starting to calm down. I thought of yesterday's storm, and the clean rain that had rolled down my cheeks, and plastered my hair against my head. The creek had run coolly over my fingertips. I wanted the service to be over and to be outside in the hot, summer air. I wanted to be underneath one of the willow trees down by the creek, where the delicate green branches fluttered in even the smallest breezes. I felt claustrophobic inside the hushed sanctuary with its green carpet and orderly pews. I didn't want to pick at the scab of my fears, over and over. I wanted to spend time in places and with people who didn't scare me, or teach me that I was bad. I wanted Tante Tina, and couldn't wait for Monday to return to her farm.

When we got home, my mom was making lunch. I set the table without being asked while Mary Anne fed Chris and my dad changed out of his Sunday suit.

As I placed the forks and knives beside the plates, I wished I didn't have to go to Canaan in September. I wanted to go to the public high school. At Peninsula High no one would know – or care – about Mary Anne and Chris. I could study real literature, not just the Bible. And I wouldn't have to hear over and over again that I was bad, that I had to get saved.

"Mom," I said, bravely, "I'd like you to consider letting me go to Peninsula High next year." Next year sounded far away, but it was already well into August.

Mom turned toward me and sighed, pushed some of my hair out of my eyes. "I guess it'll be just one more thing your dad and I don't agree on," she said. "But we'll talk about it."

I felt bad that I was going to cause more troubles with my parents, but it felt right to know what I wanted.

PICKING WILD BLACKBERRIES

The next day was Monday. I packed up my clothes as usual – some shorts and T-shirts, a light raincoat, nothing else – and came down for an early breakfast. Usually my dad was the only one up. He worked the early shift on Monday, so we'd eat breakfast together, then drive to Tante Tina's house.

This morning, however, my mom was in the kitchen. She had on a pair of jeans and a long-sleeved shirt, and a kerchief over her head.

"What's the occasion?" I asked her.

"I'm going berry picking today. The wild blackberries are ready. They make the best jelly."

The best jelly, and the most heavenly syrup – thick, purple, and sweet, delicious over ice cream. My mother's berry patch had always been a secret, her private spot like my willow tree sanctuary.

"I'd like to take you there," my mom said.

Maybe she was trying to be extra nice to me after our Friday night conversation when I wished I was Tante Tina's daughter.

"You probably think I'm a pretty good picker now that Tante Tina's trained me," I said to my mom.

"I'm probably right, huh?" she said to me, smiling like a friend.

"What about you, Dad? Can you tell the General you've gone berry picking?" Part of me wished he would come with us. We rarely did anything fun together these days. But I knew he would go to work as usual. It couldn't be easy being the father, being the man who always had to report to the General, no matter what.

"The General doesn't abide a lazy man," my dad answered. "You know that."

I saluted him, smiling.

But my mom got mad at him. "Picking berries is not being lazy," she said, untying and retying her kerchief. "It's hard work! It's hot and the bushes are prickly and you have to crawl around on the hillsides. I always get cut!"

My dad shook his head, as though he couldn't believe what he was hearing. "But you like it," he told her gently. "You love picking berries."

Through my mom's anger shone a quick, radiant smile. "Yes, I do love picking berries," she admitted.

My dad gave her a kiss on the cheek. "And I love you."

My mom swatted his shoulder, but smiled again. Both my dad and I were relieved.

My mom packed up a few buns and some cheese and my dad drove us to Tante Tina's on his way to work. He said he would pick Mom up on the way home. We sat quietly on the way there. It was so early the sun was just rising, an orange-pink sphere that woke up and hovered over the blanket of horizon before getting out of bed and stretching itself into the sky.

Tante Tina was in the barn milking Klempie when we arrived. My dad waved goodbye as he left. My mom didn't see him. She just walked in big strides over to the barn, calling "Tina! Tina!"

Tante Tina's forehead was pressed against the warm flank of Klempie. Her hands squeezed and pulled, directing rhythmic squirts of milk into the pail. The bucket foamed beneath her hands. She turned toward my mother and looked surprised, but pleased to see her.

"*Nah,* Alma," she said without stopping the milking. "Today I get two for the price of one? Are you staying all week too?"

"Just for one special day, Tina," my mom said, girlish and excited. "Today I want to take you and my Tina berry picking. I know just the spot!"

Tante Tina smiled at me. "What did we do to deserve this?" Until now my mother's berry patch was her well-guarded secret.

I shrugged and shook my head, but inside I knew why my mother was trying so hard to be nice to me. It made me feel a little bad. I often said things when I was angry that I regretted later.

Tante Tina finished milking Klempie and got up

from her milking stool. She picked up the bucket of warm milk in one hand, and said, "I'm all for berry picking, but milk waits for no man. This milk has to be separated before we go anywhere!"

It was my usual Monday morning chore and I didn't mind it a bit. I think my mom was surprised to see me work so hard without any fuss. I followed Tante Tina into the kitchen and set up the separator. We poured the milk in together and I cranked and cranked, getting hotter and hotter, my face flushed and pink.

Tante Tina filled the coffee percolator and soon the smell of coffee reached my nose. The thought of having a cup of coffee when I was done made me crank faster and faster, and pretty soon I had a bucket of skimmed milk and a lovely pitcher of thick, sweet cream.

What a feast we had then! Tante Tina liked a dollop of fresh cream in her coffee, and we all ate cream with *zwieback* and jam.

As soon as we finished breakfast, we piled into Tante Tina's station wagon. My mother gave directions and brought us to a place near the escarpment where blackberry bushes grew thick along the creek, which ran beside a set of old train tracks. It was my creek – only closer to its source, above most of the farmland and orchards.

Here it ran cool and green beneath a line of old oaks and the biggest willow tree I had ever seen. It was like a waterfall. Its branches rose from the trunk and cascaded down the tree in skirts like water, casting liquid, green shade that was breezy and refreshing.

Tante Tina parked in the shade and we climbed out of the station wagon. My mom had brought margarine containers and one large plastic bucket. "For some reason the berries grow good here," she said, handing us each a plastic container.

We walked toward the creek where the berry bushes grew. The spiky branches were thick with berries, like Christmas trees decorated with too many ornaments. Below the berry-filled banks, the creek gurgled and murmured. What a nice spot. I smiled at my mom, but she wasn't looking. She was already halfway down the bank picking berries.

I started picking too. The thorny branches scratched my wrists, so I tried to be very careful, reaching in and pulling off berry after berry. There were lots of berries and they fell into my plastic bucket with satisfying, hollow plops at first, and after a while there was no sound. Tante Tina found a spot a little farther away, and when I looked at her, she smiled at me and waved.

My mom was a fast picker. She filled her container first. Then she started on another one. By this time it was midmorning. We were all sweating. My mom and Tante Tina wore kerchiefs on their heads that absorbed the sweat, but my perspiration dripped down the sides of my face. One drop even rolled off my nose into the basket of berries.

I put my bucket down in the shade of the black-berries and went to Tante Tina's car. I knew there would be a Thermos of ice water underneath the driver's seat. I pulled it out and took a swig, wiped my forehead with the back of my hand, and took another swig. Nothing tasted as good as plain, cool water on a hot day.

Tante Tina saw me and smiled. I brought her the water and she took a drink, smacked her lips and said, "Ah," then took another gulp.

"Do you want some water, Mom?" I asked.

"Not thirsty," she muttered without looking up.

"What do you mean, you're not thirsty? It's about a hundred degrees out here. Here, have a drink."

"I'm not thirsty," she insisted, pulling blackberries off the bushes with both hands. She was nearly finished her second bucket, and I still hadn't finished my first. How could she pick so many more than me?

"I just don't stop," she said, as though she read my mind. "That's the secret."

"*Nah*, Alma," Tante Tina said. "Is there a race I don't know about?"

"We're just here to pick berries!" my mom said, irritated. "So why don't you do that instead of chatting and drinking and wasting time!"

This was the way my mother was about chores. She wouldn't stop until they were done. Tante Tina worked differently. She took little breaks throughout the work. She looked around her, told stories, told me the names of flowers and birds. I preferred Tante

Tina's way. When you had a lot of work ahead of you, it didn't hurt to stop. Rather, the stopping fuelled you and allowed you to finish the job. This way the job never seemed too big, or too boring. Which is about how the berry picking started to look to me.

I picked up my plastic bucket and started pulling berries off their branches, but it wasn't fun any more. I wandered down the bank toward the green creek. The sumac bushes wore reddish candle tips that would flame later at the end of summer. A nut tree dropped pebbly green nuts that smelled like lemon when you scratched their shells. Tall thistles wore purple caps, but the milkweed pods were still too green to open. Their leaves oozed a milky white sap that stuck my fingers together. It smelled green and bitter. A monarch butterfly hovered around the milk-weed. I heard a woodpecker hammering hollowly in the trees and a dragonfly shimmered blue and stared at me with huge, round eyeballs.

I heard crackling and turned around to see Tante Tina approaching the creek. *"Nah ja,"* said Tante Tina. "I think I need some shade. That big willow tree looks like it's waiting for us to sit down under it."

The breeze waved the willow branches like magic wands. They seemed to say yes. We sat with our backs toward each other, with the great willow trunk between us. Above us, my mother continued to pick. I knew she would be angry, and I wished she would join us.

I heard plopping sounds as frogs jumped from creekside mud into cool water. Butterflies spiralled in double helixes around pink flowers.

"Look," Tante Tina said quietly, and directed my gaze at a leaf on the ground.

"What?" I asked her, and she pointed again.

I looked harder and saw that it was a praying mantis, green like the grass and leaves, its back streaked with grey that hid it from view. Leaves above us rustled in warm gusts of wind. Squirrels chattered above us and were silent again. The praying mantis had huge round pink eyes and when I looked closely, I could see myself reflected many times.

We sat quietly for a while, and then I said, "I'm going to go back to Mom. She probably wants my company too." I picked up my bucket and climbed the hill, picking berries as I went, finally filling my first bucket. At the top of the hill, beside the car, my mom was putting down her third bucket!

"It's lunchtime," I said.

My mom looked at me and shook her head. "So now I see why you like to work with Tante Tina. She doesn't work you as hard as I do."

"Well," Tante Tina said coming up behind me, "we still get everything done."

"Yeah! And we have fun."

"Fun," said my mom, as though the word tasted strange in her mouth. "Fun," she said again, as though the strangeness of the word started to feel more comfortable to her.

"Yeah, fun!" I said again, and laughed. "Remember fun?"

My mother closed her eyes for a minute and smiled sheepishly while shaking her head. "Fun," she repeated. "I tried to give you everything a mother should give you, and that's what I missed – fun!"

"That's okay, Mom. You sent me to Tante Tina and she gave me fun." It felt funny to comfort my mother, to reassure her that she was a good mother.

I put my arm around her and walked toward the station wagon where Tante Tina was preparing our picnic lunch. She sliced tomatoes and cucumbers and set out buns and cheese. She had found some wild onions and they spiced our sandwiches with their tangy flavour. In a second Thermos she had hot coffee, which we drank happily, though the day was hot too.

For dessert we had a handful of berries, though my mother frowned, and then we picked some more. Even my mom picked more slowly now. The sun peaked in the summer sky, then started its lazy descent along the arc of afternoon. It was the time of day I liked the most – when much of the day's work was done and the evening was still ahead, promising conversation and stories and companionship.

When the day turned the corner to late afternoon, we finally stopped picking. The three of us formed a bucket brigade to bring the berries to the back of the station wagon. We had picked nearly ten buckets.

"The jam will last past Christmas, anyway," said my mother, half-heartedly admitting that we'd done a good job, even though we'd had fun.

SECRETS

The rest of the week was my last week with Tante Tina. Already. I couldn't believe summer was almost over. I didn't know if my dad would agree to send me to Peninsula. I started thinking about all my troubles and I wished this week with Tante Tina would last as long as eternity. But only the bad things lasted forever. Good things always ended too soon.

I wasn't very good company that day, and I even snapped at Tante Tina, something I'd never done before. She looked at me hard, and sent me to play with the kittens in the barn.

"When teenage girls are in a bad mood, they need to be alone," she said. "My girls were like that too."

I took a book to the hayloft and read with my lap full of kittens. By dinnertime, I felt better, but it was hard to fall asleep and when I did I dreamed the dream that I hated. When I woke from that dream, still half asleep, I got up and walked to Tante Tina's bedroom, and stood in her doorway.

Her breathing was even and slow, and filled the room with a feeling of safety. I don't know how long I stood there, listening to her breathe, when suddenly I heard her voice.

"*Miale*," she whispered. "Don't just stand there like a ghost. Come lie down beside me."

"I had that dream again," I told her.

"Tell me about it, *Miale*."

I couldn't answer at first.

"What's the dream?" Tante Tina prompted.

"I'm on a beach and there's an old man with me, and he tells me I have to pick up every grain of sand off that beach. He says I have to put the sand into a pail. I have to do it, have to do it, and I know I can't do it. But he says I have to!"

"*Nah,* who is he?" asked Tante Tina.

"I don't know," I lied. I knew it was my Opa, but I didn't want to say.

"Is it God telling you what to do?" Tante Tina asked me.

I shook my head.

"Is it your dad?" she asked. "A teacher, the prime minister, a preacher?"

I shook my head beside her. "I don't know," I repeated stubbornly.

"Well, then, that's easy to fix," said Tante Tina. "Next time you have that dream, change the ending. Make the old man disappear. Have fun on the beach instead."

"I can't change it," I protested. "I'm just dreaming."

"It's your brain, isn't it? You can tell your brain what to do."

"But I don't get it," I said. "If I can tell my brain what to do, what part of me is telling my brain? I thought my brain is what does the telling."

"Nah ja, Miale," Tante Tina laughed. "You make it too complicated. Just pretend it's going to be easy, that you can do it. And next time you have the dream, change the ending! It's like writing a story."

For the first time, it didn't seem like Tante Tina was helpful. I just wanted her to hug me or stroke my head and say everything was going to be all right. Now she wanted me to do something difficult. All of a sudden I felt like a grown-up, like I had to take care of my own problems, and it made me feel small and scared.

We lay quietly for a moment. Her breath became even and slow again, and I found myself floating on it. I began to feel sleepy and safe.

Then she said, "Is the old man my brother?"

I didn't answer, but tears came into my eyes. She had guessed right.

"What did he do to make you dream of him like this?" she asked me gently.

I didn't want to tell her, but I wanted to say it. I wanted to get the ugly secret out of my head where it kept me awake at night, and out of my heart where it was so big that Jesus didn't have any room.

I took a deep breath and a sob caught in my chest and hot, fat tears rolled out of my eyes into my ears.

"You can tell me," she said. "Remember all the things I told you when you asked, even though I didn't want to. You know all my secrets."

I wanted to talk, but I couldn't force words out of my throat.

She began to hum a nonsense song with made-up words, all about a cuckoo sitting in a tree, *"Zim zalla dim bam bazala-doozala dim,"* she sang.

The silly words made me laugh through my tears.

"It won't be so bad," she said gently. "It will feel better to tell this secret. Secrets like this just make you sick."

She was quiet then, waiting for me to speak.

When I finally did it, it was so easy that I wondered why I had waited for so long.

"He stuck his hands down my pants," I said. "And he touched me where no one's supposed to touch. We were inside his barn. I don't know where my parents were. I don't know why my dad wasn't there to stop it. It's not fair. Nobody leaves Chris alone like that. Why did they leave me alone with him? Where were they? I hate him and he smells bad. He's so mean and miserable. Why does he kill kittens and why did he do that to me? I wish someone would stick him in a sack," I was sobbing now. "And drown him too! And now he's going to come and live at our house. I won't live there with him!"

Tante Tina took me in her arms. She was warm and soft. Her hair was long and it felt like veils. She held me tight and let me cry. She touched her cheek to mine and my tears rolled down her face.

Sitting there in Tante Tina's arms, I remembered the thing I didn't want to remember. I had been alone with my grandfather that one time. My dad had left me with him in the barn while he went into the garden to help with something. My Opa sat down on a hay bale with me on his lap. He started to absently stroke my back.

I felt like a cat in his lap, trapped. Why didn't I get up and leave? I was just trying to be a good girl! To do as I was told. I was afraid to insult him, to make it seem as though he was doing something wrong.

But as his hands began to curve around my back and touch first my ribs, then my stomach, and up under my arms and around to the front of my chest, I began to panic. This couldn't be happening, I thought. Then I wished for the woodsman in *Little Red Riding Hood,* the one who killed the wolf with one stroke of his axe, to come and save me. I waited for the axe to crash through the wood of the barn door, the woodsman pulling me off my Opa's lap, making me safe.

But no woodsman came. My Opa continued to hold me tight against him. I was trapped.

I thought then about a fairy tale my Oma told me in German, when I was a child, about a wolf who tricked a family of goats whose mother left them alone at home while she went out to find food.

This wolf covered himself in flour and knocked at their door. When they called, "Who is it?" he said he was their mother. They peeked out the door and when they saw the white figure they opened the door. The wolf rushed inside and ate all of the kids except the smallest one who hid in the clock cabinet. When the mother goat came home, shocked at the absence of her kids, the littlest one came out of hiding and told his mom what happened. Together they went into the forest and found the wolf, who by this time was so bloated and full that he had fallen asleep.

I remembered relishing the thought of the mother goat slicing open the wolf's belly and replacing her rescued kids with rocks so that when the wolf woke from his nap and went for a drink of water, he fell into the river and the rocks dragged him down so he drowned.

I wanted someone to do the same for me, to catch my grandfather and stuff him full of rocks and let him fall into the river. But then my Opa's hands moved across my ribs toward the soft flesh of my stomach. His fingers brushed the little buds of my breasts. Then he moved his hands down my body and slid them into the waistband of my pants.

The pants were too tight and he became angry, and tore the waistband and moved his fingers inside my panties. I felt like throwing up. I was confused. I was angry with my Opa, but angrier still that there was no one to protect me.

Where was the woodsman with the big axe who saved Red Riding Hood? Where was the mother goat?

"Why isn't life like the fairy tales?" I wailed to

Tante Tina, who stroked my hair and let me cry. My face was crushed into the soft heft of her generous chest and her nightgown was damp from my tears.

His hands were calloused, and the skin on his fingers was rough. His touch felt like sandpaper. He began to make noises then, as though I was a pigeon and he was calming me. I remembered wishing for a sharp beak to peck him with and wings to fly away. But I sat there, frozen, his one hand imprisoning me against him, his other hand trespassing. Silently I screamed for my dad, and called for my mom, but no one came. I was trapped.

As Tante Tina rocked me, a thought long-buried slid across my brain like the headlights of a car across a dark wall through a window at night.

I hadn't waited for someone to save me. I wasn't ever as helpless as Little Red Riding Hood and her grandmother. I had twisted around in my Opa's lap and shook his hands off my body and stood up abruptly, and had run for the door.

I got away, away from the smell of mould and decay and loneliness and fear that surrounded the old man. His whiskers were white against the pale skin of his aged face, I remembered, and his eyes were startlingly blue and red-rimmed as he looked at me, surprised.

Now, held safely by Tante Tina, I said aloud, "I am the coachman. I am the woodsman. I am the little kid in the clock!" Held tight in Tante Tina's arms, I finally understood the true meaning of fairy tales. I could feel the weight of the woodsman's axe in my own hands. I felt the strength of the coachman's words as he saved Onkel Thiessen's family from the soldiers. I felt the terror and the exhilaration of the little kid hiding in the clock waiting for the right moment to come out.

She didn't say anything, just let me cry. After a while, my sobs turned to hiccups. That made me laugh. Slowly I stopped crying. Tante Tina turned the lamp on, and I was surprised to see that we were sitting on the side of her bed. I had forgotten where we were.

"How about some hot milk with honey and cinnamon?" she asked.

Her voice was soft and low and broken, and I could see that not all the tears on her face were mine.

She wrapped a housecoat around herself, and I went to my bedroom and did the same. When I came to the kitchen, the milk was in a pan. Tante Tina's hair was messed up at the back from where it had tangled around me, and I straightened it out with my fingers while she stirred the milk.

We didn't say much then, only sipped the sweet milk. It was too early to stay up, and I started yawning. Tante Tina yawned too.

"You can sleep with me if you like," she said to me.

But now that the secret was out and I had remembered that I was strong, I wasn't afraid any more. I wanted to be in my own bed.

"I'm fine," I told her. "Really. I'll see you in the morning." I felt shy after all that honesty. I felt strong and courageous too.

"*Schlaf gesund, Kindlein,*" she said to me, which meant sleep well.

"*Gute Nacht,*" I said to her, which meant good night.

We were both quiet the next day. I felt peaceful, and a little tired. Tante Tina looked older, worried, thoughtful. Maybe it was lack of sleep, but it might have been the weight of my secret. I felt lighter for the unburdening, but now she carried some of it too.

HANGING LAUNDRY

The rest of that week was quiet. We picked and packed peaches, made some *glomms,* and a few people dropped in for cream. The peach fuzz and humidity made us itchy and irritable. The realization that it was my last week with Tante Tina didn't make things any better.

When my mom came to pick me up on Friday, Tante Tina asked me to clean up some baskets in the barn and she went inside the house with my mom. I didn't know what they were talking about, but when my mom called me to come to the car, she was upset. I could tell because she started the car and backed out of the driveway fast without waving to Tante Tina. I did, though. As I waved, I thought Tante Tina looked upset too. I wondered if Tante Tina had relayed my secrets, but my mom didn't mention anything.

My dad wasn't home when we got there. He had gone to church early tonight, to help prepare the bread and grape juice, and wash and dry all the little glasses for a special Communion service. He seemed to go to church more often now, as if he was making up for the rest of us not going.

As soon as we got home, my mom went downstairs to do the laundry.

"Where's Mary Anne?" I called down the stairs.

"She's gone to look at a place for rent," my mom called back, her voice sounding muffled and faraway.

I went to my bedroom and sat on the bed, feeling funny and lonely. Nothing felt familiar or secure to me. I lay down on my blankets for a moment and shut my eyes. Inside my head it was dark and my heart pounded strangely.

Then my mom called from the basement. I got up and went down the stairs to the laundry room. She had a mouthful of clothespins and indicated with a nod of her head that I should help her pin the wet clothes onto the line. We worked together silently and when she emptied her mouth of pins, she spoke.

"Tina," she said, and I got a funny feeling in my stomach at the tone of her voice.

I looked at her carefully. "Mom?"

"I have to tell you something important. I've wanted to tell you for a while now. I think you're old enough to hear this. And I have to tell someone."

I waited. My stomach felt like butterflies were playing badminton. What was she going to say? I was afraid to hear it, but when she spoke the words, they weren't as bad as I thought.

"I don't believe in God anymore."

I looked at her with wide eyes and didn't say anything.

"I mean, I believe there is a power," she continued. "But it's not like what they teach us in church. It's not something you can describe easily. It's not a bearded man who sits in heaven watching us through a telescope. It's not someone who is going to send us all to hell as soon as we step out of line."

I looked at my mother without saying anything. So she doubted too. That was a relief. I wasn't alone. She continued to hang wash until the basket was empty. Then, her hands empty, she looked at me. Finally I reacted, and gave my mother a hug. She hugged me back.

"Tina," she said. Her voice was quieter now, timid even. "Tante Tina told me about Opa. I feel terrible. I feel angry and scared and madder than a big, angry bull." Her voice trembled. "If there was a God like the one they preach about, there might be some true retribution when old men do terrible things to innocent girls."

I didn't know what to say. "It's all right, Mom." And it was all right. I had the power of the woodsman inside me now.

She hugged me again and as she held me I asked her, "Does he have to come and live here? Couldn't he go to the old folks' home?"

She nodded. "I'll figure out some way to tell your dad. Meantime, let's be glad the secret is out, the story is told."

I agreed.

We went upstairs and sat at the kitchen table. Potatoes were boiling in a pot. I could smell a ham roasting in the oven. My mother had washed lettuce for a salad and the greens decorated the dish rack like a bouquet.

Mary Anne and Chris came home. The house started to feel like my home again. Chris was roly-poly and smiley and I held her on my lap and made her laugh while Mary Anne prepared her bottle. My dad was still at church.

Everything was normal, and nothing was ever the same again.

The terrible fears I'd harboured, and the guilt that came from not believing, left me. I felt light now that I wasn't the only one who didn't believe. My mother's confession made me feel like they always told me I'd feel when I got saved – forgiven, released, freed. And I was glad my secret was out.

My mom washed her hands in the kitchen sink. She broke lettuce into a bowl, cut tomatoes and cucumbers. I handed Chris over to Mary Anne and set the table for all of us. I spread a tablecloth as if it was a special occasion. My mother and I were a little shy with each other in the kitchen. We spoke very politely to each other, as though we were strangers.

I lit two candles, turned off the overhead lights, and called Mary Anne to the table. She was surprised to see the fancy setting. She put Chris in her seat on the table beside her. Chris seemed to like the candles, and waved her hands and crowed.

Before we started eating, I broke one of my mom's *zwieback* in three, spread them with butter and offered them around, like communion. Then I poured us each a glass of my mother's homemade grape juice and added a splash of ginger ale. We toasted each other and giggled in the candlelight.

"What do you think of this, Tina – do you suppose you'd like to go to Peninsula High School in September, rather than Canaan?"

My mother was full of surprises today!

Would I? "Would I!"

Mary Anne smiled. "See, I knew she'd be happy," she said to my mom. Chris seemed to sense that we were all happy. She smiled too, making a sharp calling noise that sounded like a cheer.

We all laughed at that. We raised our glasses of ginger ale that were bubbling in the candlelight. When we clinked our glasses together Chris crowed again.

My dad came home then, surprised to see the candles. He turned on the kitchen light as a reflex and my mom said, "Oh, Werner! Do you have to spoil our fun?" And then our fun was spoiled.

"Come have some ginger ale, Dad," I said. "We're celebrating."

"What's the occasion?" he asked us.

It was hard to describe what we were celebrating. I couldn't tell him that it started because my mom said she didn't believe in God. That would make him just as sad as it had made us happy. I couldn't tell him about Opa. It felt too strange to do that now, in the harsh glare of the overhead light.

Then I remembered school and I said, "You and Mom are the greatest! Mom just told me you decided I could go to Peninsula High in September." I wanted to say something to tell him I loved him.

"That makes you so happy?" he seemed incredulous.

"You bet!"

As happened so frequently and easily, Chris's crowing and smiling turned to tears. She was hungry. Mary Anne gave her a bottle and she quieted down. I poured my dad some ginger ale and my mom blew out the candles.

"Silly," she said. "Candles when the lights work."

She gave my dad a nice smile. I knew she was trying to be nice to him, to make amends. He picked up his glass of ginger ale and I made him clink against my glass in a toast.

THE DREAM

The next morning my dad left early for work. As he left the house, Chris was yelling about something. Mary Anne was up too, looking through the paper, trying to find a place for them to rent. I got up and ate breakfast and made my bed, and after that I had a vague sense of uneasiness in my stomach. I thought everything would be all right after last night, so I was surprised that I felt so uneasy.

I dusted the furniture without being asked. My mom started a batch of *zwieback* and called thank you from the kitchen. Then I changed my sheets and tidied my room and lay on my bed reading for a while, but I didn't feel like being inside. The feeling inside my stomach was too big for the house, so I put on a big sweater and headed to the creek.

The early September sun was warm, a little watery as autumn approached, and the wind was cool in the morning. Down by the creek the willow leaves sported bright yellow patches, promising golden fall colours. I sat down with my back against the tree trunk, behind a curtain of willow branches.

Sheltered from the wind, I felt protected, and warm. I was sitting in sunlight, felt the light all around me and inside me too. I closed my eyes. There was light behind my eyes too, a waving kind of light. The shifting willow branches in the sunlight must have been throwing shadows. I guess I fell asleep, because all of a sudden I was sitting on a beach and I felt the uneasiness in my stomach turn to terror.

Then a shadowy form in the distance approached me. I tried to scream, but couldn't force sound out of my throat. The figure came closer; it was my Opa. He set a bucket down in front of me and I knew what I had to do. It was all so clear. He didn't have to say a word.

My eyes had a special light in them that made me see everything perfectly, my hands, the pail, the water, the sand. The sand was numberless, infinite. I could see too that I didn't want to obey him. Why should I pick up all that sand? It belonged on the beach. Anyway, what could he do to me? I didn't move.

He came closer. He waved a walking stick at me and shouted. His white hair blew around his face and he looked like an angel. Not a good one. I looked around for someone to help me, but there was no one, nothing on the stretch of empty beach except the bucket, waiting for me to fill it.

My Opa's face was angry and his mouth was a hole that sucked the light out of my eyes. I tried to keep my light, but his mouth was like a magnet.

When almost all my light was gone, I started to feel dizzy and slumped onto the sand. And then the bucket was in my hand. I didn't want to look at my Opa, but he stood over me. I hated him, and his black mouth sucked the strength out of my muscles. I got angry then, and I lifted my hand and threw the bucket at him. It hit him right in the mouth and a couple of pigeons flew out of him and fanned the air with their wings. Then they landed on his head and he started melting, just like the wicked witch in *The Wizard of Oz*. He turned into liquid that poured into the bucket, but when I looked, the bucket was empty and so was the beach.

I struggled to open my eyes. It felt like they were welded shut, but I pushed hard against sleep, and when they opened, I was looking up at the sky through a lashing of willow branches that shifted and shimmered in the light and wind.

All I could think of were my mother's *zwieback*, hot and golden in their pan, waiting for me to add a dollop of jam and devour them. I got up slowly, first onto my hands and knees, and shook my head to try to clear the images from it. Then I pulled myself up, holding onto the willow tree to steady myself, and started walking home.

The familiar streets of my neighbourhood seemed strange today. The ordered yards seemed too neat, the driveways too straight.

When I got home, our house was empty. The little buns sitting in their pans on the countertop were the only signs that people lived in the house. The oven was still warm and the house smelled like fresh buns, but there was no note, nothing to say where everyone had gone. The car was missing from the driveway. The house was quiet without Chris's constant chattering.

I had been left behind! I looked in Mary Anne's room to double-check, but it seemed fairly obvious. No one was here. Jesus had come back. The Second Coming had happened while I was dreaming about killing my Opa, and of course I had been left behind. I felt sick and went to sit in my dad's Lazy Boy chair, but that didn't feel right, so I then tried my mom's rocking chair. I felt like Goldilocks, but nothing was just right.

I felt hungry, so I went to the kitchen and broke open a bun and ate it plain. The inside of it was soft like the communion bread prepared by the deacons in the church basement. I'd never taken communion, because I wasn't baptized, but it felt right to eat my mom's *zwieback* plain like that when I was so afraid.

Then I went to the phone and dialed Anna's number. Her father answered after two rings. He had a very soft phone voice and a very strong accent, and he told me that Anna had gone to her Oma's house for lunch. I hung up the phone, relieved. If Anna's father was still here, then maybe Jesus hadn't come. Anna's father was a good Christian – he wouldn't be left behind.

Relieved, I sat back down in my mom's rocking chair and rocked and rocked myself, like I was in the swing with Tante Tina. I thought of calling her, so I dialed her number, but there was no answer at her house. Maybe she was out in the barn. I knew that Klempie was pregnant and due soon. I pictured the cow stall, warm and manurey, smelling of hay and milk. I began to feel a bit better.

The curtains at the kitchen windows swelled with late summer breezes. The cicadas in the trees outside the house buzzed and rang. Their song intensified until it was so loud I covered my ears. Then it petered out and the world was silent again. Too silent.

I remembered that the car wasn't here. If Jesus had come, my parents wouldn't have left in my dad's Pontiac LeMans. I rocked myself some more and almost fell asleep in the rocking chair, but I sat up with a jolt when the phone rang. It was my mother, calling from the Hotel Dieu Hospital in St. Catharines. At first she was angry at me.

"Where were you, Tina? We called and called for you, but we couldn't wait!"

"I went to the willows," I said, and she cut me off.

She told me that Opa was dead. He had suffered a heart attack in his barn and died with only his pigeons around him. Tante Tina had discovered him when she went to visit him. I wondered why she had gone for that visit. Had she perhaps confronted him with my story? Is that why he had the heart attack? I wondered if it was all my fault. Maybe I had killed him.

"Chris is fussing," my mom was saying to me. "We're going to come home as soon as we can." My dad had left work early and was making arrangements to take care of the body.

I sat back down in the rocking chair and rocked and rocked myself, until my stomach felt queasy again and I stopped. I felt like a murderer. I was a murderer. The cicadas buzzed and rang in agreement.

When I let myself think about it, I realized that I didn't really care that the old man was dead. And then I felt guilty and my stomach ached and squirmed and the bottom of my body felt as heavy as concrete.

I did feel sorry for my dad. It was his dad. How would I feel if my dad died? I didn't want to think about that.

I remembered my dream and I felt strange, like I was connected to angels or – worse than that – devils. I had to get out of that rocking chair so I went to the kitchen.

They'll want a snack when they get home, I thought. So I boiled eggs, got out the farmer's cheese, and laid slices of ham and salami on a plate, decorated it with pickles, and made strong black tea, the way my dad liked it, with milk in the pot, and sweetened with white sugar. Then I put the pot on the back burner on low heat and tried to read a book.

By the time they got home, I felt more like myself again. The fear had left my stomach, moved up somewhere behind my heart. The house filled with sound again. Mary Anne went to her bedroom to put Chris to bed. I followed her. Chris was already asleep and looked like an angel. She opened her eyes and yawned and smiled when Mary Anne changed her into sleepers and fell asleep immediately. She was so content that I began to feel safe too. We turned out her light and tiptoed out of the room.

Tante Tina was in the kitchen. She seemed to fill the room with light and warmth. She hugged me and put her forehead against mine. Then she turned me around by my shoulders, and held me against her, and said to my dad. "Well, Werner...." and then she faltered. Tante Tina, usually so vocal and strong, couldn't tell my dad. I kept my eyes down.

I wasn't ready to tell him. Not yet anyway. My mom was quiet too.

"Well, Werner, let's sit down, shall we?" said Tante Tina, recovering.

We all sat at the kitchen table, not saying much, just asking for buns and tea and cheese and pickles. No one could find anything to say about my Opa. Some of us had secrets about him. Some of us knew each other's secrets. I don't think my dad knew any of it. He was just quiet and a little sad.

We ate the food and sipped sweet, milky tea. If my dad wasn't there, I might have told them about my dream.

"This is a very nice snack," said Tante Tina. "I guess Tina has learned a thing or two from me." She winked at me and smiled and started talking about Klempie. She was good and pregnant. There would be lots of milk in the spring. I remembered that Tante Tina had lived through famine and war. Plenty of milk was important to her. We laughed at the story of Mietze who was supposed to keep the barn free of mice but was frightened by a rat that was almost as big as the little cat. I shivered at the thought of the big rat.

After a while things felt almost normal again. It was nearly midnight and I was sleepy.

I kissed my mom and dad and Tante Tina, and even Mary Anne. They all smiled at me as I went to my room.

Tante Tina got up from the table and followed me.

"I had a dream," I told her. She sat beside me on the bed. The little lamp beside my bed made shadows beneath her eyes and turned her into an old crone. Her crown of braids looked like a turban and she looked like a fortune teller.

"So did I," she said.

I shivered again and got under the covers.

"You first," she said.

"I dreamed of Opa. He was forcing me to do something I didn't want to do," I said. "So I threw a bucket at him and he disappeared."

She laughed abruptly and shook her head. "In my dream," she said, "I was in the cow barn, trying to milk Klempie. But I couldn't find the bucket. Klempie was full of milk, mooing and lowing at me. I searched the barn, but the bucket was nowhere."

We were both quiet. Then she laughed, silently because it was late. Her heaving shoulders shook the bed. I thought I was in a boat on a stormy lake. It was weird, but it wasn't that funny.

"I guess you had my bucket," she said when she stopped laughing. "I was so angry at that bucket. If I found it I was going to give it a good kick." She chuckled again. "So much happens that we can't explain," she said. "That's good."

She turned out my light, but stayed on my bed. I could hear her breathe beside me.

"Do you think I killed him?" I whispered into the dark.

She snorted. "That's what I wanted to do to him! That's why I went over to see him this morning. But he was already dead! I was sorry for only one reason – that I couldn't tell him once and for all what I thought of him! I guess his heart just stopped. That's what the doctors at the hospital said. He was old and that's what happens."

We didn't say anything for a while. Tante Tina leaned over and stroked my hair. "I hope your bucket's back in the barn," I whispered as I fell asleep.

I didn't hear her leave.

THE FUNERAL

Opa's funeral started with a German service in church. After that my mom and dad, Mary Anne, Chris, and I got into my dad's Pontiac LeMans and drove to the cemetery behind a long black hearse with the coffin in the back. A procession of cars followed us. All the other cars turned their headlights on, although it was the middle of the day.

I was surprised to see how many people attended my Opa's funeral. It was important to Mennonites to attend the funeral of one of their own and to show support for our family.

The grassy cemetery sat on a flat piece of land near Lake Ontario. At the edge of the cemetery, on its journey to the lake, flowed Willow Creek. In sharp contrast to the neatly tended cemetery, the sumac and towering oaks along the creek were wild. Tall, unmowed grasses at the creek's edge swayed in the afternoon breeze. A weeping willow wore a few slashes of early autumn gold in its flowing green. I looked up as I followed the crowd to my grandfather's grave.

A high cirrus cloud painted the sky with a brush stroke of white.

The coffin, decorated with a bouquet of dark red roses on a background of ferns, was already placed beside the grave. A white ribbon spelling Father in silver letters was draped across the flowers. Piles of white and red carnations, potted yellow daisies, and fat purple chrysanthemums brought a look of celebration to the graveside.

I stood with my mom and dad, Mary Anne, Chris, and Tante Tina on one side of the grave. A green carpet that was supposed to look like grass lined the hole where the coffin would be lowered. Many people from church and Orchard Road joined us, bowing their heads when the minister said, "Let us pray."

When we lifted our heads, I looked around. Some of Mary Anne's church friends approached her and admired Chris. There was an air of forgiveness today. Maybe the reminder of death encouraged people to be kind.

My dad looked serious but not sad. He shook hands with all the people who offered condolences. I was proud of him. Though Tante Tina didn't go to church, she seemed to know everybody. She was telling stories and laughing just as usual.

My mom, however, was quiet. She had not forgiven the church people for their disapproval, and for their cold shoulder when Chris was first born. And she hadn't forgiven my Opa. She stayed near my dad and shook hands with anyone who came near, but didn't say much. In fact she hardly looked up. If you didn't know better, you might have thought she was very sad about my Opa. I knew that she was angry.

Slowly all the cars left the cemetery. Everybody drove back to the church where the cooking committee ladies brought out platters of sausages and baskets of buns and their husbands brought out the big bowls of coleslaw. People took their seats around the long tables and the funeral turned into a feast.

A mens' quartet sang a hymn in four-part harmony. Though they sang hymns, the singers were very vibrant, smiling while they sang. I liked the man with the big moustache and twinkling blue eyes who sang bass. Their funeral songs were strangely jubilant. They rejoiced about my Opa's new home in heaven. I hoped there were pigeons there, and that the other people in heaven didn't expect him to make great conversation.

After dinner it was the *Freiwilliges* section, the unplanned part of the program. An old man went to the front and told a story about my Opa when he was a young man in Russia before the war. He spoke in Low German and, as always, the language brought out the humour in these usually serious people. My Opa, he said, had been a stamp collector, and the old man told a story about driving a carriage to another town with my Opa to find a special stamp. The old man cleared his throat and looked down at his hands and then he added that my Opa's interest in stamps might have had something to do with my Oma, whose father collected the mail from the Mennonite villages and took it to the main city once a month. The people in the church basement laughed at this comment, and then the quartet sang another song.

I was surprised when an old lady told a story of how my Opa was proud of me and Mary Anne when we were born. We were his only grandchildren and he treasured us. It was hard for me to believe that. My mother tightened her lips and I was afraid for a minute that she would stand up and shout out my secret, but she stayed quiet and stared down at her plate.

Then Tante Tina spoke. I couldn't imagine what she was going to say. Would she tell stories about him now that he was dead and gone? Would she tell them how he killed the Polish peasants during their terrible trek through the war?

"Many of you," she began, "know that my brother and I feuded." She looked around the room at the nodding heads, and continued. "I won't say why here, even though I know you wish I would! But what I do want to say is that I understand why he was the way he was, why he did the things he did, why he was forever changed after the war."

I saw a whole bunch of old people nodding when she said this. Maybe Tante Tina and my Opa weren't the only Mennonites with bad memories and bad blood from the war and that long and terrifying flight from Russia to Germany.

"I forgive him," said Tante Tina, "for whatever he

did that made me so angry at him. Maybe it doesn't matter now that he's gone, but it's important to clean the slate so that the young ones will grow up with some good memories of him. The young ones like Tina and Mary Anne and Chris."

I watched as people around the tables nodded at each other.

I hadn't noticed Onkel Thiessen in the crowd of people, but all of a sudden I saw that he was being helped to the front. He spoke in such a hoarse, low voice that the room got quiet and hushed. "I knew him when we were both young boys," he began. It was hard to imagine either my Opa or Onkel Thiessen as young boys. "We loved to go fishing and climb trees." Just like me! "He liked *Spass,*" continued Onkel Thiessen. My Opa's sense of humour was news to me. "We used to knock on an old bachelor's door," said Onkel Thiessen. "Then we ran away and hid and laughed to see the old man come to the door and shake his cane in the air.

"I was taken to a work camp in Siberia," continued Onkel Thiessen, when the chuckles subsided, "and I didn't see him for many years. When I got out, the war was over and my family was gone. So much sadness, such tribulations. For all of us. When I saw my boyhood friend next, he was a changed man. The war," said Onkel Thiessen, "and that terrible flight from Russia to Germany through Poland affected him in some strange way."

Onkel Thiessen's voice was very quiet, but everybody in the room was listening. Some people wiped their eyes. My dad looked proud and sad at the same time. Tante Tina was nodding her head. Mary Anne smiled at me. Only my mom still looked down at her plate. I could see that she didn't forgive him, even after these nice stories. Part of me was thankful because I knew she was mad at him for me.

The next day was Labour Day, the day before school started. I felt sadness every year at this time. This year it was more pronounced. My wonderful summer with Tante Tina was over. The freedom of summer would soon have to be traded for the routine of school. I would be starting Peninsula High, a new school, with new teachers, and new students. The idea of such change made me happy and scared at the same time. And it was sad to think of leaving Anna behind.

"I'm excited about going to Peninsula tomorrow," I told my mom. "But I'm a little scared too."

"Why don't you go visit Anna," she suggested.

I set out immediately. Other farm families had to work in the orchards today because it was the height of harvest season, with apples, pears, and grapes ripe and ready to pick, but Anna's father decreed that his children would have one last holiday before school started. And what a day! The high, hot sun of summer had mellowed to gold. The cloudless sky was a deep shade of blue. I walked to Anna's farm along the creek where wild pear trees shed their ripe yellow fruit. The grass at creekside was tall and curving and starting to dry.

Anna and her sisters were just finishing the lunch dishes when I arrived. "Let's go outside," she said. I agreed. First we went to the barn and filled our pockets with crisp red apples. Then we headed down the orchard road toward the creek.

"Let's go barefoot," said Anna. I knew she was thinking about school starting tomorrow. About black jumpers and pantyhose. We pulled off our sneakers and socks, hiding them in the crook of a tree to pick up on our way back. The lane was sandy and dry. Fine dust like flour puffed up beneath our feet as we walked. If you looked closely, you could see tiny dust fountains erupting between our toes. The peach and cherry trees on one side of the road were bare, and the leaves on these trees were starting to dry and turn brown. On the other side of the road, bright red apples still decorated their trees like Christmas decorations. The pear and plum trees would need picking soon. Full clusters of grapes hung from their vines, ready to be cut, releasing the sweet scent of grapes into the warm air.

At the end of the rutted lane, the orchards gave way to wilder, tangled trees. Oak leaves were starting to turn rusty brown. The sumacs' candle flames were fuzzy and red. The milkweed pods had cracked open, allowing little bits of silk to float out of them onto the warm air. The willows at creek's edge still had leaves, but they were turning yellow. They rustled in the afternoon breeze. Waist-high grasses on the creek banks bowed and swayed in the wind.

Without saying anything we both sat down in the grass, and then stretched out full length, flinging our arms above our heads and wiggling our toes. We crumpled the grasses beneath us, but the grasses above us covered and shaded us and waved above us like autumn pennants.

"I like autumn best," Anna said.

"I like it all right," I replied. "But it's so sad. Everything is dying. And it feels like I'm dying a little too."

The willow branches stirred and swayed above us. I looked up and it seemed as though they were dancing with the sky. I thought of my mother's friend Lily. She would have her baby soon. Rose if it was a girl. Chris and Mary Anne would soon be living on their own and I would be alone with my parents, who didn't seem to want to be alone together.

I heard the plop plop of little frogs at creek's edge. Crickets creaked rustily and then stopped as soon as they had started. Just practising. Everything rustled and crackled gently. I felt the breeze ruffle my hair.

"Get up," said Anna, "I want to braid your hair."

I sat up and she knelt behind me and combed my hair with her fingers. She parted my hair from my crown down to the nape of my neck, separated each side into three strands, and made braids. I bowed my head a little and felt her fingers in my hair and the sun shining softly on the skin of my neck.

With my eyes closed I could hear the breeze rustling in the tall dry grasses. The willow branches sang like wind chimes above the fluid running of the creek.

The next day was my first at Peninsula High. I woke up early enough to see the sun rise. I ran down to the creek for a quick visit to my favourite willow trees. Then I ran home. The house was filled with a delicious but unusual smell when I walked in the front door.

"What are you making, Mom?"

"French toast," she said, as she flipped another piece into the pan. "I thought I'd do something different for such a special day!"

I hugged her. Then my dad walked in the kitchen, with his hair neatly combed with Brylcreem. I could see the tracks the comb had left. The kettle whistled and my mom turned to pour a cup of coffee for my dad.

"I'll have one too," I said.

"Oh, you will, will you?" My mother hesitated for a moment, and then she prepared another cup for me. I guess she agreed that I was old enough now.

We ate together. I was nervous, but not so bad that I couldn't eat. I felt brave and ready to go to a new school.

"Are you going to leave your hair like that?" my mom asked me.

I touched the braids Anna had made yesterday by the creek. "Yeah. It's a new style," I replied. I wanted to keep the braids that reminded me of my good friend and everything that was familiar.

My dad drove me to school. In the future I would take the bus. Peninsula High School was out on the highway, on the outskirts of Homer. All the kids from the farm district went there. Some of them I knew from elementary school, before I went to Canaan, but many of them would be strangers.

For my first day of school I wore jeans and runners, a T-shirt and a jean jacket. I felt perfectly me. I wondered who I would meet, and what I might learn. I expected adventures, new friends, and freedom, so much freedom. My dad turned into the parking lot. It was full of cars. Yellow school buses discharged students in front of the two-storey red brick school.

Before I got out of the car, my dad handed me a leather bookmark. On it was written, "Is a candle brought to be put under a bushel, or under a bed? and not to be set on a candlestick? (Mark 4:21)"

"That's just to remember who you are, and who we are, and what's important," he said. And then he hugged me. I wondered if anybody else was getting hugged like it was the first day of Kindergarten, but I hugged him back generously. Then I got out of his car and headed across the parking lot toward the double doors, joining the stream of students entering school. I didn't turn around and wave, but walked straight ahead.

ACKNOWLEDGEMENTS

I wrote the first chapter of this book when I was 17, gazing out my bedroom window, across a swath of peach orchards, over the choppy blue waters of Lake Ontario, to the distant, miniature skyline of Toronto. The book itself was completed more than 17 years later in a small hamlet in the Rocky Mountains. The dream of writing this story came to life as a result of much work and many helpers – my list of thanks is long! Elementary school teachers Judy Tassonyi and Pat Kilgour, high school teacher Pat Malkiewich, and Ryerson professor Stuart Maclean all provided positive feedback on my early writing. Pure, unadulterated magic from the spirits of Baja, Mexico, and Cahuita, Costa Rica, catalyzed inspiration into writing. Absolute faith from a shining star, Letty Grant, lit my way when it was darkest. Therapist Allison Butts Magnusson helped me learn to believe in myself. Friends Cate, Sueby, Peggy, Paddy, and Margery did best what girlfriends do – talk, talk, talk! How could I not write when Mandi kept saying:

"Write on, sister!" Money generously supplied by the Alberta Foundation for the Arts allowed me the free time to sit and write. My colleague in conservation, Bart Robinson, showed me by example the secret to good writing (a comfortable chair and eight hours a day!). Though they've shaken their heads and rolled their eyes, they have loved me steadily and teased me gently, and for that I thank my wonderful siblings: Sister Brigitta, Peter (Nutman) John, Hermano Roberto, Eduardo el Magnifico, and a cuppa Joe. I cannot imagine life without them! Nor can I imagine it without tout le little gang: India, Marty, Lucas, Simon, Nicole (who has so much to say), Gabriel, and Kai. To the mountains who shelter me, strengthen me, and keep me cool all year round, I give a ringing round of applause. A daughter's thanks and love go to Susanna whose stories helped shape this book, whose patience helped ground me, and whose armwarmers kept the blood circulating as I typed. To Peter who taught me to forgive, I offer my gratitude and respect. For filling the everyday with superbly expressed no-holds-barred love, I thank fellow writer and partner-in-life, Stephen Legault (although how does he expect me to get any writing done with all those kisses?). To Geoffrey Ursell and Coteau Books, appreciation for a good eye and a steady hand. And to editor Barbara Sapergia, hats off for helping me shape 17 years worth of inspirations and longings into this story of which I am superbly proud!

ABOUT THE AUTHOR

Kathleen Wiebe lives in Harvie Heights, Alberta, on the perimeter of Banff National Park, where she works as an administrator for the Yellowstone-to-Yukon Conservation Initiative. *Willow Creek Summer* is her first published book. Born in St. Catharines, Ontario, Kathleen grew up in Niagara-on-the-Lake. She lived in Costa Rica for a time, where she worked as a freelance writer for *Tico Times,* that country's English-language weekly newspaper.